DEATH RIDES THE HIGH PLAINS

"You two need to haul your freight back east in a puffin' hurry."

"Why was that old fart deliberately trying to scare us?" Julius asked. "Sure we had a couple of nasty set-tos with those bounty hunter chaps. But I've seen no sign of them since then. We—"

Fargo raised a hand to silence him. "You've missed all the signs because you won't stop batting your gums. Men who survive out here keep their mouths shut and their eyes open. Look over your right shoulder. See anything?"

Megan, too, looked. "Nothing," they replied together.

"Well, you're both wrong," Fargo informed them. "Dead wrong. Dust puffs have been trailing us for at least two miles. Somebody's coming to kill us."

THE TRAILSMAN
#301

HIGH PLAINS GRIFTERS

by

Jon Sharpe

A SIGNET BOOK

SIGNET
Published by New American Library, a division of
Penguin Group (USA) Inc., 375 Hudson Street,
New York, New York 10014, USA
Penguin Group (Canada), 90 Eglinton Avenue East, Suite 700, Toronto,
Ontario M4P 2Y3, Canada (a division of Pearson Penguin Canada Inc.)
Penguin Books Ltd., 80 Strand, London WC2R 0RL, England
Penguin Ireland, 25 St. Stephen's Green, Dublin 2,
Ireland (a division of Penguin Books Ltd.)
Penguin Group (Australia), 250 Camberwell Road, Camberwell, Victoria 3124,
Australia (a division of Pearson Australia Group Pty. Ltd.)
Penguin Books India Pvt. Ltd., 11 Community Centre, Panchsheel Park,
New Delhi - 110 017, India
Penguin Group (NZ), cnr Airborne and Rosedale Roads, Albany,
Auckland 1310, New Zealand (a division of Pearson New Zealand Ltd.)
Penguin Books (South Africa) (Pty.) Ltd., 24 Sturdee Avenue,
Rosebank, Johannesburg 2196, South Africa

Penguin Books Ltd., Registered Offices:
80 Strand, London WC2R 0RL, England

First published by Signet, an imprint of New American Library,
a division of Penguin Group (USA) Inc.

First Printing, November 2006
10 9 8 7 6 5 4 3 2 1

The first chapter of this book previously appeared in *Backwoods Bloodbath,*
the three hundredth volume in this series.

PUBLISHER'S NOTE
This is a work of fiction. Names, characters, places, and incidents either are
the product of the author's imagination or are used fictitiously, and any resem-
blance to actual persons, living or dead, events, or locales is entirely
coincidental.
   The publisher does not have any control over and does not assume any
responsibility for author or third-party Web sites or their content.

The Trailsman

Beginnings . . . they bend the tree and they mark the man. Skye Fargo was born when he was eighteen. Terror was his midwife, vengeance his first cry. Killing spawned Skye Fargo, ruthless, cold-blooded murder. Out of the acrid smoke of gunpowder still hanging in the air, he rose, cried out a promise never forgotten.

The Trailsman they began to call him all across the West: searcher, scout, hunter, the man who could see where others only looked, his skills for hire but not his soul, the man who lived each day to the fullest, yet trailed each tomorrow. Skye Fargo, the Trailsman, the seeker who could take the wildness of a land and the wanting of a woman and make them his own.

High Plains, Kansas Territory, 1860—
where Judge Lynch presides and
Fargo is invited to a social—a hemp social.

1

Skye Fargo stood in the shadow beside his hotel room window, keeping a wary eye directed outside on the ramshackle livery barn at the far edge of town.

Since entering the Kansas Territory three days earlier, he had been followed by two young Southern Cheyenne bucks. Because most Plains Indians were partial to pinto horses, and Fargo rode a top-notch pinto stallion, it seemed likely they meant to boost his Ovaro.

Cheyenne, he knew, were not town fighters. Sneaking into a livery in broad daylight, however, to steal a white man's mount would count as a great deed and earn them coup feathers. So Fargo had slid open the sash and had his brass-framed Henry rifle propped against the wall nearby. He had no intention to shoot for score, only to kick up plenty of dust and send the braves running.

Fargo wore fringed buckskins, some of the strings stiff with old blood. His crop-bearded face was tanned hickory-nut brown, and the startling, lake blue eyes had seen several lifetimes of danger and adventure. He cast a wider glance around the once-thriving town of Plum Creek.

"Boom to bust," he muttered, amazed by the rapid change.

The last time the Trailsman, as some called Fargo, rode through Plum Creek, the place was fast and wide-open. Seemed like everybody had money to throw at the birds. But he had watched plenty of boomtowns turn into ghost towns practically overnight, and clearly this berg would soon make the list. Last night a rough bunch of buffalo-skinners had made enough ruckus to wake snakes. The hiders were gone now, and the sleepy little crossroads settlement seemed on the verge of blowing away like a tumbleweed.

There was still this hotel, though, Fargo reminded himself, even if it was the size of a packing crate. And even more surprising, a bank straight across the street. That was especially hard to believe—Fargo had played draw poker the night before with a few locals, and all but one had used hard-times tokens as markers, private coins issued by area merchants to combat the critical shortage of specie.

Again Fargo's gaze cut to the livery, but the Ovaro was peacefully drinking from a water trough in the paddock. Fargo watched sparrow hawks circling in the empty sky. The only traffic in the wide, rutted main street was a despondent-looking farmer driving a manure wagon.

Until, that is, a fancy fringed surrey came spinning around a corner near the bank.

Fargo whistled appreciatively when he'd gotten a good look at the driver. "Well, ain't *she* silky-satin?" he asked the four walls of his cramped room.

The surrey pulled up in front of the bank in a boil of yellow dust. The Trailsman forgot about the two Cheyenne, dumbfounded at this vision of loveliness. The young woman on the spring seat was somewhere in her early twenties, with lush, dark-blond hair pulled straight back under a silver tiara and caught up under a silk net on her nape. Hers was a face of angelic beauty except for full, sensuous lips.

Fargo had an excellent view, and with his window open he heard everything that transpired.

"Yoo-hoo, young man!" she called out in a voice like waltzing violins. "Yes, I mean you. Come here, please."

A slight, puzzled frown wrinkled Fargo's brow. Her accent, he guessed, was supposed to sound French and might fly in these parts. He'd heard better imitations, though.

A boy of about twelve years of age, a hornbook tucked under his arm, was just then passing along the raw lumber boardwalk. At the woman's musical hail, he turned to look at her and his jaw dropped open in astonishment. Like Fargo, he seemed mesmerized by the gay, ostrich-feather boa draped loosely around slim, white shoulders, and the way her tight stays thrust her breasts up provocatively.

"Yes, you," she said again, laughing at his stupefaction. "I don't bite!"

"Hell, a little biting might be tolerable," Fargo muttered.

"Please run inside the bank," she told the awed lad, taking a coin from her beaded reticule, "and tell them an invalid lady requires help outside."

"Yes, muh-muh-ma'am!" the kid managed, staring at the coin she placed in his hand.

Invalid? Fargo's eyes raked over her evidently healthy form. It was early September, dog days on the High Plains, and the still air felt hot as molten glass. Yet the mysterious woman's legs were wrapped in velvet traveling rugs.

Fargo's vague suspicion of the beauty instantly deepened. He was familiar with the ways of grifters, and it didn't take him long to twig the game. No traffic outside, the bad French accent—and her noontime arrival when only one teller, probably the bank manager, would likely be on duty. Suddenly he recalled one of Allan Pinkerton's detectives telling him about how the "beautiful invalid" scam worked with surprising ease at small-town banks. Gallant managers were eager to run outside and cash small bonds or redeem stock coupons, leaving the bank briefly unoccupied.

Sure enough, one dashed out now, resplendent in pomaded hair, a new wool suit, and glossy ankle boots.

"Your servant, Madame," he greeted her, even tossing in a clumsy bow.

"*Now* I see which way the wind sets," Fargo muttered, a grin touching his lips.

The sheep was about to be fleeced, but the Trailsman had no intention of stepping in just yet. This was going to be a good show and Fargo, mind numbed by his long ride across the plains, needed the diversion. However, he resolved to recover and return the money later—the citizens of Plum Creek were poor as Job's turkey and could ill afford a loss. Besides, that course of action allowed him to see the woman up close. In this territory, females like her were only seen in barroom paintings of Greek and Roman nymphs.

"Sir, you are *so* kind!" the striking young woman effused. "I have been in your wonderful country for only six months, and I am—how you say?—puzzled about bonds. May I ask a few no-doubt silly questions?"

"Madame, *nothing* you ask could be silly," the bank officer assured her.

Fargo shook with mirth while the deceitful shill, as he assumed her to be, removed some papers from a wallet. As the two conferred, heads intimately close together, Fargo watched behind them for the woman's partner. Yet, even knowing what was coming, Fargo's eyes were almost deceived.

The sneak thief was impressively adept at swift, silent movement. Like a fast shadow he glided out of an alley and onto the boardwalk, soundless in the cork-soled shoes of his trade. He slipped inside the bank so quickly that eagle-eyed Fargo hardly gained an impression—only that the small, dapper man's hair was silver at the temples and his fox-sharp face was slightly puffed and lined.

"And what is this," the woman's lilting voice inquired, "about ac-cum-u-la-tive interest? *Ciel!* Such a difficult word!"

Fargo laughed outright, admiring the little sharper in spite of her criminality. Right now, while the bedazzled bank manager stood in a stupor, the sneak thief inside would spend less than two minutes rifling the open vault. If the vault was closed, or yielded little, he would leap to the cash drawers. Then he would unlock the rear door and make his escape.

The moment the woman reined her two-horse team around and headed back out of town, Fargo went into action.

He buckled on his heavy leather gun belt and palmed the cylinder of his single-action Colt to check the workings before he snatched up his Henry. He trotted down to the livery, tacked the Ovaro, and swung up and over, reining in the direction of the surrey's dust trail.

Not surprisingly, the conveyance was making jig time as the couple tried to avoid capture. For the Ovaro, however, it was swift work to carry Fargo alongside. The "invalid" was no longer driving, that job falling to her male partner. Keeping his eyes on both, Fargo leaned out and grabbed the reins from the man, drawing back to halt the team.

The beauty's nostrils flared in anger. "Sir! I protest! My father and I are in an urgent hurry!"

Fargo, grinning like a butcher's dog, let his eyes sweep over her. "Well, pardon me all to hell. Sweetheart, you really need to polish that phony accent. Sounds like you got a bad head cold."

"Phony?" she protested. "It is the way we speak in Par-ee, but, *mais oui*, of course a benighted savage like *you* would not know this."

Fargo took in wide, emerald green eyes with thick lashes that could flutter most men into total submission. She had flawless skin like creamy lotion, and a figure that would tempt a saint to impure thoughts—and Fargo was no saint.

However, the Trailsman was forced to shift his attention to her companion, whose right hand was inching toward his vest. The man was compact and well groomed, in his forties, with distinguished silver streaks in his hair, a neat line of silver mustache, and shrewd, intelligent eyes that missed nothing.

His hand moved another inch and Fargo said mildly, "Don't miscalculate yourself, mister. Just because I'm smiling politely don't mean I won't kill you if you skin that hideout gun. Real slow, toss it down."

"Now see here!" he protested in a suave baritone, his accent as phony as the woman's. "I am merely checking the time. See?"

Under Fargo's close scrutiny he slid a watch from the fob pocket of his silk vest and thumbed back the cover. "*Mon Dieu!* We are indeed tardy for our appointment, Arlette. Sir, my daughter and I have a crucial engagement and must resume our journey."

Fargo laughed. "Damn straight you must. The sheriff of Plum Creek is hard as sacked salt. Maybe you've heard of the Kansas troubles? This whole region is known for hemp socials, and 'trials' take place a few minutes before the hanging. Even for genteel bank robbers like you. True, even here they won't hang a woman, but *you* will decorate a cottonwood."

"Bank robbers! How preposterous! We employ neither masks nor guns, the tools of that nefarious trade."

"If it chops wood," Fargo assured him, "you can call it an ax. You talk like a book, mister, and I don't trust flowery men. Now shuck out that hideout gun, nice and easy."

The girl calling herself Arlette tossed back her pretty head and laughed, showing Fargo even little teeth, white as pearls. "*You*, sir, are in my bad books," she coquetted.

Fargo knew it was just a desperate bid to distract him so her companion could get the drop on him. Fargo's Colt leaped into his fist. The loud click, when he thumbcocked it, made both grifters go a shade paler.

"Cottontail, you can play that bank manager like a piano, but I know women like he knows ledgers. Now, mister, hand it over, and don't try a fox play or I'll let daylight through you. That's something I'd surely hate to do, by the way."

The man's veneer of cool composure now cracked completely. Scowling, he handed Fargo a two-shot derringer with a folding knife under the barrels.

"Now," Fargo added, "hand over that buckskin pouch that's on the seat between you."

"Sir," the man protested, his face going red with anger, "yours is the manner of a man who holds the high ground and all the escape trails. *If* we stole this money, as you boldly assert, how are you any different from us? Clearly you intend to steal it for yourself."

"The hell you jabbering about?" Fargo said, growing impatient—he thought he spotted dust puffs from the direction of town. "You're lucky I'm letting you two ride on instead of turning you over to the law. Now hand over that swag and get going before I change my mind."

"You hairy brute!" Arlette flung at him. "Neanderthal! Picking on gentlemen and ladies must be your specialty!"

Fargo laughed again, glancing inside the pouch before tucking it into a saddle pannier. He tapped both bullets out of the derringer and tossed it into the surrey.

"No need to get on your high horse, missy," he said. "All I steal are kisses. By the way—both of you seem to be losing your *French* accents."

Arlette blushed to her very earlobes as the man, suddenly cursing out Fargo like a dockworker, removed the whip from the surrey's socket and lashed the team into motion.

Fargo headed back toward Plum Creek and quickly realized his mistake—the bank robbery had been discovered almost immediately because that was definitely a posse thundering right at him. He had figured to return the stolen money before the alarm was raised. Banks never reported a robbery if they could recover the money without publicity.

Possibly a witness had seen him leave town in a hurry. The Plum Creek sheriff, Hinton Davis, had kept a wary eye on Fargo last night, and Fargo had seen him pocketing payoffs from the town's few remaining sporting gals. He didn't strike the Trailsman as a by-the-books lawman. And the "good citizens" with him right now, Fargo realized with a sinking heart, looked more like a hemp committee than a posse. He recognized several scurvy-ridden toughs who had been in the saloon last night.

"Well, old campaigner," Fargo said to the Ovaro, "looks like I put our bacon in the fire again."

The moment he fell silent, still trying to decide what to do, the whip-crack of a rifle sent ice into Fargo's veins. That first shot hissed wide, but within seconds more bullets hummed past his ears like blowflies, some so close he felt the tickle of wind-rip.

The moment of stunned immobility passed in a blink, and the will to live instinctively asserted itself. He still had a full magazine in his sixteen-shot Henry, and six beans in the wheel of his walnut-gripped Colt. This was no time, however, to make a stand. That jackleg posse was coming at him like the devil beating bark, and clearly they had no plans to arrest him. Nor was Fargo willing to kill any of them—after all, it was his legal duty to report, or stop, the bank theft, not let it play out for his amusement.

"Fargo, you damned knucklehead," he cursed himself

as he clawed the buckskin pouch from his pannier, "I hope you enjoyed your little diversion."

However, he didn't toss down the pouch as he'd intended. Fargo knew that Davis and his minions would give up the chase quickly once they had the money. The initial excitement would be over, and they were townies. However, Fargo also believed this bunch would split the swag, not return it to the bank. He would send it back to Plum Creek by express rider first chance he got.

Fargo reined the Ovaro around, kicked him up to a gallop, and lowered his profile in the saddle. Fearing for the two grifters, he veered off the road and led the vengeful pursuers toward more rugged terrain, bullets thumping the ground all around him.

2

"Ain't that the beatingest, hoss?" 'Bama Jones wondered aloud. "All them dough-bellied peckerwoods from town tryin' to salt the tail of that hombre in buckskins. Why, you reckon?"

Reed McKinney snorted like a horse deep in the stream. "Old son, you musta been wiping your ass with both hands when they passed out brains. Don't you recognize Skye Fargo? Most likely that tomcat got caught with the wrong queen."

"Fargo, huh. He could be one o' them whatchacallits, a bad omen," 'Bama mused with a frown. "His stick floats one way, ours the other. Ain't he one o' them crusaders?"

"*I'll* tell the world," Reed assured him. "But he's a one-man outfit, not some soapbox reformer."

'Bama was a man mountain, six feet five and two hundred fifty pounds, and had killed men with just one blow from his mallet-hard fist. A thick, wild, dark red beard grew past his chest.

His partner Reed, in striking contrast, was small but sinewy tough, with gimlet eyes and a hard, cruel mouth. The bounty hunter preferred to gut a man with the eleven-inch bowie in his sash, although he was a crack shot with the Colt .36 Navy pistols in rawhide holsters tied low on his thighs.

"Hey, think I saw something," Reed put in, squatting to get a better look at the retreating Fargo. They had found a good position behind a spine of rocks. Reed hurried to his horse, an ugly paint with powerful haunches. He took a pair of stolen U.S. Army field glasses from a saddlebag.

"I'll be damned, I was right," he told 'Bama moments later. "Quick, have a look-see. He's got a buckskin pouch shoved kinda half-assed into a pannier—and I'd bet my guns that's the same pouch the Kinkaids are using to carry away their bank hauls."

When Reed offered the glasses, 'Bama grounded a revolving-barrel shotgun that, in his capable hands, could clear out a canyon. He studied Fargo a few moments.

"Be damned," he remarked, lowering the glasses. "Reed, you ain't thinkin' Fargo's in with the Kinkaids?"

Reed, his sunburned face blackened by thick beard stubble, pulled on his chin, conning it over. His lips twitched back off his teeth like a wolf's.

"Hell, who knows?" he finally said. "Fargo ain't no scrubbed angel, and brother, Megan Kinkaid could get a rise out of a dead man."

'Bama's flat, turtle-eyed face look troubled. "Damn the luck. Could be he's a bad omen for us, all right. But the old hogleg here will do for him, Reed."

'Bama preferred his sidearm to double as a club, especially with ammo of the day being notoriously unreliable. So he wore a Colt Third Model Dragoon, one of the heaviest Colts known. The steel of its case-hardened frame weighed even more with a metal backstrap.

Reed dismissed his comrade with a sneer. "I ain't met him, but you can ask any jasper who roams the West. Skye Fargo fights like a she-grizz with cubs. He's slow to rile, but once he gets blood in his eye there's generally a funeral."

"I can kill him, hoss," 'Bama repeated, his tone wheedling now. "Ain't nobody stopped me yet."

Reed cursed in disgust at his simpleton, kill-crazy partner. 'Bama was from a big but poor clan whose patriarch had decided which babies were thrown to the hogs at birth. For years it was young 'Bama's job to do the actual tossing, and now his entire career as a bounty hunter was a quest to rediscover that earlier excitement, power, and fascination of killing. Anyway, that's how Reed figured it.

Still, he needed a stone-cold killer like 'Bama. The

huge man could neither cipher nor write, but he sure-god knew the science of killing. Both men were also excellent trackers, like Fargo, well versed in stealth and ruthless in pursuit. Both were always well horsed and could live off the land. When resupply of mounts or ammo became a problem, they simply murdered travelers and homesteaders. Honest men feared them, but the law ignored them.

And right now both of them were closing in on Julius and Megan Kinkaid, a father-daughter heist team who currently went by the handles of Jacques and Arlette Lagasse. A team so effective at sneak-thievery that they rated a ten-thousand-dollar reward, dead or alive.

"Let's just hold our horses," Reed said abruptly. "Might be we figured this bass ackwards. Fargo was headed *in*to town, right, when them boardwalkers commenced to chuckin' lead at him?"

'Bama looked confused. "Yeah, so?"

"Jesus, bo, think on it! Bank robbers *leave* town. The Kinkaids musta hit the Grangers Bank in Plum Creek while we was still cuttin' sign on 'em. Fargo caught 'em somehow and took the money, meaning to return it. I hear that's just his style. Ain't likely he's in with them two."

'Bama sighed, on the verge of pouting. "Oh. Yeah, all that rings right, don't it? So I don't get to kill him?"

"That ain't the main mile, you clodpole. The point is we prob'ly won't have to plant Fargo to get at the Kinkaids—he'll save his own ass and cut his tether from them. Even so, Julius is trouble enough, and his daughter ain't no calico rose."

Reed paused, picturing the headstrong young beauty from New Orleans. "Way I see it, all cats look alike in the dark. But I mean to get my ration from Miss Megan before we kill her, and brother, *that* little piece just might spoil me for ugly women."

'Bama scoured the vast terrain with the field glasses. To him, women would do to kill, but he had no more use for them. "Think them Injins is still out there?"

A shadow passed over Reed's face. "Hell yes, they're out there. Them's two Cheyenne from south of the Republican River."

"Republican Riv—" 'Bama gaped. "You mean where we—?"

"Ig-*zac*-ly. Where we wiped out that camp of squaws and whelps last winter. Or was it spring?"

"Katy Christ." 'Bama added, "So they ain't after Fargo?"

"Does your mother know you're out?" Reed barbed. "They're just keepin' an eye on him. It's *us* they're after, bo, and you seen that charcoal streaking their faces. Black is the color of death. You don't have to sit on the benches at West Point to know that's trouble."

Reed pointed below, where Fargo and his pursuers looked insect-size. "We can thank Fargo for drawing off the posse. C'mon—we're burning daylight. Let's hit leather and go calling on the Kinkaids."

3

At first, as Fargo lit a shuck to the north and the more rugged country around the Arkansas River, he expected this chase to be another coffee-cooling detail. But Hinton Davis and his unsavory crew hung on like ticks, leading Fargo on a merry chase across the High Plains of the Kansas Territory.

When he reached the timbered ridges overlooking the Arkansas, Fargo reined in to study the tableland rolling out below him. He backhanded sweat from his brow and saw the posse was in ragged formation now, their tired mounts blowing foam.

"We broke 'em, old war horse," Fargo said, patting the Ovaro's damp neck. "But, Jesus, they rode like Comanche, hey?"

It was only late morning when Fargo and his pinto began that close escape. Now the afternoon was well advanced.

"Still coming," Fargo marveled. "But they'll soon give it up as a bad job."

The Ovaro, too, was blowing hard, so Fargo hid in a steep erosion gully until his pursuers had finally pointed their bridles south again. With his shadow beginning to slant toward the east, Fargo headed into the sand-hill country—good cover in a scrape. He had no idea where the two "French" grifters were by now, but thanks to them—and his own stupidity—Fargo was in possession of stolen bank loot.

Suddenly curious, he slid the buckskin pouch up onto the saddle and untied the flap.

13

"Nine hundred dollars," he muttered. "Figured my hide was worth more."

Still, it was a good haul for a day's work—a typical laborer, out west, was lucky to earn fifty dollars a month. This was a year and a half's wages.

The Ovaro whickered a warning, and Fargo immediately scanned the rolling brown terrain surrounding him. To his east the Great Plains stretched toward infinity, still virtually untouched by the plow. It dwarfed a man, all this open space and no way to get your bearings, but also gave a good view of any hostile observers.

Such as the two Cheyenne braves watching Fargo from at least a thousand yards out. They boldly sat their ponies, making no attempt to hide.

"Yes, I see you, gents," Fargo remarked calmly. "If it's my horse you want, he's spent. But I'm not."

The wind swirled, shifting directions again, and the Ovaro caught the Indian scent. He lifted his head sharply, ears pricking forward. Fargo stroked his neck and spoke soothingly, letting the stallion continue into the sand hills at an easy trot. Fargo knew full well what those two braves wanted him to see: both carried coup sticks dangling with scalps, and the red-painted hands on their ponies indicated many kills.

Fargo wasn't all that sure anymore that the Cheyenne did indeed want his horse. They were taking too long to make an attempt. Instead, they seemed only to be watching him, as if deciding what manner of man he might be. They had yet to actually threaten him.

Within minutes, however, Fargo had a new distraction— the sound of a man and woman hotly arguing up ahead.

No French accents now, but he recognized the voices. Fargo threw the reins forward and swung down, sliding his Henry from its saddle boot. He crouched and scuttled over a line of barren hills, getting a perfect view of Arlette and her companion.

"You old fool!" the woman flung at him, her words etched in acid. "If you hadn't let the bearded buttinsky see you enter the bank, I wouldn't be sleeping in a Santa Fe bed tonight."

"You're lucky you're not whoring on Gallatin Street,"

the dapper man shot back. "Complain all you like; these bank cons beat the prospects back in New Orleans."

Fargo winced when she slapped the man so hard he lost his bowler. "*Lucky* I'm not whoring—that's how you talk to your only daughter? I'd be married to the district attorney if *you* could have controlled your Irish temper! I'll show you 'lucky,' Daddy dear."

She lit into her father with a barrage of fists. He tried, futilely, to defend himself. Fargo grinned and stood up, intending to end this dustup before the girl killed him.

A heartbeat later, however, somebody beat him to it. Two men, one crouching like a gunman, the other a massive figure toting a revolving-barrel shotgun, rounded the shoulder of the hill behind the grifters.

For a second something about them seemed familiar to Fargo. He was astounded at the dapper gent's agility and the woman's speed. The man spotted them and leaped aside just in the nick of time—the giant with the turtle eyes discharged his shotgun, sending up a geyser of sand right where the father had been standing.

All this happened in mere moments. The woman snatched a Colt Pocket Model from her bodice and opened fire. But Fargo was no longer a spectator—that shotgun blast had opened the ball, and murder was the obvious goal. He worked the Henry's mechanism, shooting from the hip.

Hot brass rained at Fargo's feet. It was a battle of raw nerve at close range, the racket deafening. Fargo turned sideways to reduce his target, spraying lead at the two attackers below, making sure they couldn't relax enough to get well-aimed shots off.

"Not the time, 'Bama!" shouted the man who dressed and moved like a gunfighter.

With that, both men disappeared behind a sand hill. Moments later Fargo heard the three-beat rhythm of galloping hooves.

He trotted down the hill. "You two all right?"

"Thanks to you," the woman replied, not bothering with the bad accent.

She smiled slyly, watching him from caged eyes.

Seeing this, her father snorted. "Megan, this is a man resolute of purpose. Even your charms won't sway him."

Fargo grinned, watching her sensuous mouth. "Oh, I might sway, but generally I won't drop. The name's Fargo, by the way. Skye Fargo."

"Pleased," the man replied. "I'm Julius Kinkaid and this is my daughter, Megan."

"Are those summer names?"

Kinkaid laughed. "No, year round."

Fargo glanced around. "Where'd you cache the fancy surrey?"

"In a covert well outside of town," Megan's father replied.

Fargo nodded. "Let me guess: it was 'borrowed' anyhow. You had these two horses waiting. And you've got legal bills of sale for both."

Megan smiled. "Can't be too careful when you're bilking the rubes."

"There's two kinds of rubes," Fargo warned her. "The kind who won't kill you and the kind who will. Those two who attacked just now—they're no rubes. What do you know about them?"

"Bounty hunters," Kinkaid replied. "We gave them the slip in Saint Joe's and in Lawrence. But unlike others we've waltzed away from, these two get right to the killing. Did you *see* that big ape open up on me? Good thing I can still do backflips."

"They were in no hurry to kill Megan, I noticed," Fargo said dryly. "Can't you think of safer, more respectable professions for your daughter than confidence shill?"

Kinkaid's foxlike face softened. "Yes, Mr. Fargo, I had the usual dreams for her. But a few minutes spent under Dueling Oaks changed all that."

Julius Kinkaid told his story, one Fargo believed and one he had heard, in different versions, all over the West: the story of being squeezed out by money and power. When a New Orleans politician attempted to seduce Kinkaid's wife, Julius challenged him to, and won, a duel. But he was destroyed by the slain man's cronies. Until then, Julius had been a wildly successful magician and sleight-of-hand artist in the Vieux Carré or Old

Quarter of New Orleans. After the duel his performer's license was yanked, and dire poverty soon followed.

"When Bronze John"—he meant yellow fever—"wiped out the rest of our family," Kinkaid concluded, "Megan and I hit the road and headed out west for the easy pickings."

"Not such easy pickings lately," Megan corrected her father. "Not since those bounty hunters were put on us by the banks."

"*Especially* those two," Fargo emphasized. "I've never met them, but I'm pretty sure I know who they are. Reed McKinney and 'Bama Jones, two stone-cold killers. You're in for six sorts of hell from that pair. They're both hardened murderers who ought to've been hanged by now. Problem is, they're also very good trackers with no qualms about killing their quarry, so they get plenty of work."

Julius said, "You don't think we stand a chance?" He glanced at the .38 he wore openly.

"They'll pick you off like lice from a blanket," Fargo assured him.

"No need to sugarcoat it," Megan said sarcastically. "You know, Mr. Fargo, we could've gotten out of this territory quicker if you hadn't given the money back."

Fargo heated uncomfortably under his collar. "Actually, I still have it. I—"

Fargo halted in midutterance, dumbfounded. Julius and Megan suddenly held their handguns trained on him. Hell, they got the drop on him in a split second. He marveled.

"I *knew* you were a thief just like us," Megan gloated. "Now cough up our money, you tall drink of water."

Fargo laughed. "*Your* money? It belongs to the people of Plum Creek."

"Not anymore," Megan said, going behind the hill to retrieve it.

While she was gone Fargo started thinking about those Cheyenne bucks. Yes, they were evidently watching him, but could it be because they thought he had partners in the area, namely Reed McKinney and 'Bama Jones? Partners he intended to join up with? After all, Fargo had the look of a tracker, especially to an Indian.

Fargo had heard about a massacre south of the Republican River. It had happened early last spring, just at first snowmelt. Two skunk-bitten coyotes named McKinney and Jones were hired by a consortium of merchants to "clear the way" for a freight road between Fort Kearney, to the north, and the new railhead at Alton, just south of the Republican.

A small band of peaceful Cheyenne refused the trinkets and whiskey they were offered for their land. There were no witnesses to prove it, but while the braves were off on the annual buffalo hunt, the two notorious killers burned down the village and slaughtered every Cheyenne woman, child, and elder who tried to escape. What made it worse, in Fargo's opinion, was the fact that the Indian Ring, powerful and crooked politicians in Washington, were said to be in cahoots with the merchants.

"Well, he didn't spend any of it," Megan reported when she returned with the pouch.

Julius Kinkaid lowered the muzzle of his .38 but held the gun ready. "Nothing personal, Mr. Fargo. But we stole it first."

"Actually," Fargo told him, "I realize that money is small potatoes now. You two have bigger problems."

"If you mean the bounty hunters," Megan said, "we can shake them. We've outrun U.S. marshals and Pinkerton men. I have charms to soothe the savage beast known as man."

Fargo shook his head. "You're both good at what you do, but you won't shake this pair. They can track an ant across granite, and they know the West better than most men know their own wives' geography. Besides, they'd kill their own mothers for snoring."

Fargo nodded toward the chestnut mare Megan was riding. "You two seem mighty handy with guns, all right, but you're still green to the West. Look at all those silver conchos on Megan's saddle. On these open plains they reflect for miles. And does either of you know how to cover a trail or make a rabbit snare? Case you haven't noticed, ain't too many fancy cafés in this region."

Megan and her father exchanged a long glance.

"We did notice," Julius finally conceded, "how those

two nickel-chasers stick like burrs. But couldn't all the talk about them be just that—talk? After all, this is the Wild West and yarns spin big in the constant retelling."

"True, but not in this case," Fargo gainsaid. "These are two ruthless, skilled killers with no soft place in them. Even the Texas Rangers, no boys to trifle with, give them wide berth."

Fargo's eyes cut to shapely Megan. "They rape any woman they want, shoot children for sport, and follow no code. Some call them animals, but that's an insult to the wild kingdom. I know of no animal that kills for the sheer pleasure of inflicting pain."

By now Megan had lost some of her cocky demeanor. "Way you talk, this sounds personal. Sure you don't know these men?"

"I don't need to meet them to know their ilk. Observation tells me plenty. F'rinstance, Reed, the littler one—has either of you noticed his cutaway holster, or the way his rear sight was filed off so his gun won't snag coming out?"

Both shook their heads, sobered now.

"That," Fargo continued, "is a brand-new breed called the draw-shoot killer. Won't be long, you'll be seeing a lot more of them."

Megan gave Fargo a seductive smile. "Skye? Would you consider accompanying my father and me? Just until we get somewhere that has transportation back east?"

In fact that's exactly what Fargo had been leading to. Not so much for the Kinkaids—after all, anyone willing to steal the hard-earned savings of poor people deserved few breaks. But it was clear to Fargo that the pair of grifters were a magnet luring two vicious murderers—murderers who killed women and children and got away with it thanks to a corrupt government. Some accounts were worth settling even if they weren't personal.

"I'll do it," Fargo said, "on one condition: *all* that money gets sent back to the bank, and I do it."

"Preposterous!" Julius exploded.

"Psalm singer!" Megan tossed in, staring at Fargo from big, fiery eyes. "Do you preach on the side? Or is this how you steal it all back?"

"All right," Fargo said mildly. "Sun's going low. I need to ride on and make a camp. Been a long day, and I need some hot coffee."

Fargo had correctly guessed that the two city-bred thieves had no supplies. When he mentioned coffee, they alerted like cats at the smell of fish.

"And hot biscuits," Fargo added as if merely thinking out loud. "Think I have some honey left."

"Father," Megan said meekly, "there are other banks, after all."

"Not on my watch there won't be," Fargo warned.

Julius scowled but handed over the pouch. "Sir, for a man so quiet and civil, you drive a merciless bargain."

Fargo grinned, watching Megan in the fading light. "There. I guess we're all family now, huh? With a sister like you sleeping so close by, I—"

"Just make that coffee," she snapped. "You may be Sir Oracle and Daniel Boone rolled into one man, for all I care, but don't start giving orders."

"I'll make coffee," Fargo bartered, "just as soon as you rip the conchos off your saddle."

Megan stamped a foot in frustration, Julius snickered in delighted surprise, and Fargo waited patiently until, as usual, he had his way.

4

"You saw it, brother," Plenty Coups said. "The *mah-ish-ta-shee-da* on the fine stallion is not one of the killers we seek. He cannot be. You saw him battle them just now."

His companion, a subchief named Shoots Left-handed, nodded agreement. They were hidden in a dry creek bed beyond the sand hills. He lifted his chin toward the wind-scrubbed hills where the white man had stood his ground.

"Not once did he turn his back to the enemy," Shoots Left-handed said. "This is a man worthy to wear the medicine hat into battle. Whoever he is, he must be respected."

"I have ears for this. Still, a thing troubles me."

Plenty Coups fell silent. He was slender-limbed, like most Plains Indians, with a strong hawk nose and coarse black hair cut short over his eyes to clear his vision. Despite admitting that something troubled him, the Cheyenne brave kept his face impassive. Only women and white men showed their feeling in their faces, a trait most Indian warriors despised.

"This *mah-ish-ta-shee-da* fights like ten men," Plenty Coups explained, using the Cheyenne word for "Yellow Eyes"—the first whites his tribe encountered were severely jaundiced fur trappers dressed much like this man. "He has not come, as we feared, to join them. However, perhaps he will kill the two sick devils before we can."

Shoots Left-handed shook his head violently. Strips of red-painted rawhide bound his braids. An eagle-bone whistle hung around his neck, and a gaudy Presidential Medal was pinned to his rawhide shirt. This bore a likeness of the Great White Father and was one of those presented to the tribes upon the most recent treaty signing—a treaty both sides had violated before the ink was dry.

"No," he protested firmly. "The High Holy Ones who rule the clouds demand that we renew the sacred arrows. It is the Cheyenne Way. But the arrows have been stained by the blood of our people. They cannot be renewed until the massacre is avenged *by us*."

Both braves fell silent in the fading glow of a bloodred sun. To Cheyenne, the four sacred Medicine Arrows were at the center of their metaphysics. The condition of the arrows was also the condition of the tribe. If the arrows could not be renewed annually, the people must wither and die, and all memory of their existence would die too.

"My cousin, Elk Girl, hid under the dead," Shoots Left-handed said bitterly. "She saw it all. It was early in the Moon When the Green Grass Is Up. She saw how the two *mah-ish-ta-shee-da* dogs held the babies by the ankles and brained them against trees."

"And then they fled beyond Great Waters," Plenty Coups supplied, for he knew the appalling narrative well. "As cowards will after their dishonorable crimes. But now the butchers are back, brother, and I vow this: I will string my next bow with their guts."

"*Ipewa.*" Shoots Left-handed nodded. "Good. A vow is best. Our thoughts must be bloody and nothing else. But I fear you may have truth firmly by the tail—this tall warrior in buckskins may kill them first and thwart us."

The two braves exchanged a long glance in the dying sunlight. Both shared the same uncomfortable thought.

"If we kill a brave warrior who has not wronged us," Shoots Left-handed pointed out, "would this, too, not stain the sacred arrows?"

Even Plenty Coups, who earned his name by bold and reckless actions, nodded in agreement. "As you say, brother. Murder is unclean and leaves a stink forever on the murderer. But the two *mah-ish-ta-shee-das* we *do* mean to kill may kill him themselves. They are spawn of the Wendigo, true, but they are also ferocious killers."

Shoots Left-handed fell silent, turning this problem over to examine its angles. His mind conjured an image of a tall, broad-shouldered man in a broad-brimmed plainsman's hat, riding a superb Ovaro. . . .

"This hair-face," he finally said. "I think I have heard his deeds sung at the Sun Dance. The Navajos to the south call him Son of Light because he saved their children from slave chains. They say his only allegiance is to the nation of brave and honorable men. He *may* kill the two devils before we can avenge our people."

Plenty Coups scowled, seeing the grim prospect. His foxskin quiver, like his companion's, held special killing arrows of fire-hardened pine tipped with white man's sheet iron, not flint. Iron clinched hard when it struck bone and could not be easily removed. The dying would be slow, painful, and almost certain.

"Yes, certainly he might kill them," Plenty Coups said. "Especially because both men have fire in their loins for the sun-haired beauty. That will cloud their thinking and then Son of Light may kill them."

"Only *if* he joins the man and woman," Shoots Left-handed pointed out. "The singers tell how this man prefers to ride alone."

Both braves were battle leaders who sat behind no man in council, but the idea of preferring solitude appalled and even frightened them. For any Cheyenne there was no life, no identity, except through the tribe.

"He is still a man," Plenty Coups said bitterly, "and the woman a great temptation. She may light fire in his loins, too."

"Then we have only one choice," his battle companion said, whistling to a buckskin mustang nearby. "Since we cannot murder Son of Light, we must kill the butchers before he can."

Each brave said a brief, silent prayer as he touched his personal medicine and the totem of his clan.

"You want vows?" Shoots Left-handed demanded just before they mounted. He thrust his red-streamered lance out, and Plenty Coups crossed it with his. "This place hears me! From where we stand now to the place where the sun goes down, our enemies have no place to hide!"

He looked at Plenty Coups, their lances still crossed. "Brother, it matters little how brave a warrior this hair-face in buckskins is. If we fail to kill the two butchers, we dare not let him kill them. You understand?"

Plenty Coups nodded. "The *Shayiela* people are doomed if our Medicine Arrows are not cleansed for renewal. One man who is not of the People is not more important than our tribe. If we must, we will carry the stink for life—we will kill Son of Light."

Fargo watched the two Cheyenne bucks cross lances and ride out to the northeast—the same direction McKinney and Jones had fled. It confirmed Fargo's hunch: those braves were on a vengeance quest against the two bounty hunters, and now they knew Fargo was not their enemy.

Except, Fargo reminded himself, that a man was a fool to make assumptions about Indians.

"What are they up to?" Julius asked, a nervous quaver in his voice. "It's Megan they're after, isn't it?"

Fargo gave a scornful laugh, still watching the braves recede into the dark, wavering blur of the distant plains. "You're a good one, Kinkaid. You train your daughter to a life of crime and danger, but now suddenly you're worried about her?"

"I did my best by her," Julius protested.

"Pooh!" his daughter retorted. "He would have sold me himself to white slavers except he knew I'd escape and geld him."

"*Both* you two ease off," Fargo snapped. "Pay attention to things that matter and forget the rest. We've got vicious bounty hunters trying to kill us, and two Cheyenne braves watching us like cats on rats. A quick way to die out here is to fight among ourselves. Julius, let's strip the mounts and hobble 'em."

Fargo's little lecture achieved results, at first. Father and daughter quit scrapping and took the Trailsman's advice. Megan watched all around them carefully, her face brassy in the fading sunlight, while the men stripped tack and sweat-soaked blankets from the horses.

Fargo sat down in sparse, wiry grass and, peering close in the day's last light, ran a bore brush through his Colt. A wiping patch followed. Next he placed a tiny drop of gun oil on the Henry's pivot screw.

"You like to be ready, don't you?" Megan remarked. "Do you think McKinney and Jones will be back tonight?"

"Hard to call that one," Fargo admitted, checking the Henry's tube magazine for dents. "It's best to assume they will and be ready."

Megan didn't look so brash now as she studied the monotonous terrain surrounding them. "I don't understand it," she mused petulantly. "It all *looks* so pure and peaceful, so sleepy."

Fargo left that one alone. To the Kinkaids this particular locale was just a remote, wide-open place full of gullible bank managers and poorly protected money. For Fargo it formed the most critical "deadline" of all: in the grassland just east of here travelers passed the all-important ninety-eighth meridian, the rainfall demarcation line where the long grasses of the wetter east gave way to the short-grass prairie of the drier west. That line defined where the true West began and made it unique, even alien, to outsiders. It made life tougher, and thus, killing less of a stigma.

"We'll split up the guard tonight," Fargo said. "Three stints, and the guard will remain right in camp, wide awake. Megan, you take first—"

"Better give first watch to my father," Megan cut in. "He's vigilant early on, but gets too sleepy after ten p.m."

"It's true," Julius admitted. "Some bilious infection I picked up from the miasma in New Orleans."

"All right," Fargo said. "Julius first, then me, then Megan."

"Megan last?" Julius asked. "Won't that be the most dangerous watch?"

"With Indians, sure, right at dawn. But in my experience, white men attack between midnight and four a.m. Still, any shift could see trouble, so look and listen close. Stay close to the other two and raise the hail at *any* sign of trouble."

Fargo noticed something curious. The palomino Julius rode bore a large, hidebound bag tied to rope netting. It could have been disguises and props for their various grifts. Julius took it off, under Fargo's watchful eye, and laid it in the sand as if it were rare and brittle. He caught Fargo watching him and scowled.

"This is private property," Julius said, "not any bank's."

"Never said different, did I? That's a curious poke you got for it."

"It's hidebound," the former magician explained. "Weatherproof. Good for clothing, memorabilia, that sort of thing."

Fargo quit fishing, but he had heard enough to be suspicious. All three quickly ate and shared some of Fargo's canteen water. In spite of himself, Fargo grew to admire his companions' alert senses. They seemed scared but determined to survive anything hurled at them.

Fargo laid his weapons to hand, then crawled into his blankets and laid his head on the bow of his saddle. The daytime heat had been punishing, but now the evening air felt soft as the breath of a young girl. A nascent moon, white as bleached bones, appeared high in the indigo sky.

Fargo noticed all that even as his exhausted body tumbled over the threshold into blessed oblivion.

5

"Fargo! Don't shoot me! It's your turn."

Fargo woke instantly, his body still tired but his mind as clear as a mountain stream. Julius Kinkaid stood over him.

"Any trouble?" Fargo asked as he kicked off the blankets.

"I don't have your experience, but I thought I heard noises that weren't natural. Might have been nerves."

Fargo stood up and stretched his lower back. His tailbone was still sore from all that time pounding the saddle yesterday.

He picked up his gun belt and buckled it on, nodding toward the dark shape where Megan was sleeping. "Checked on your daughter?"

"I was just headed that way."

Both men stepped softly closer.

"Look at her," Julius whispered, almost fondly. "That girl could sleep through a steamboat explosion."

Megan's golden mane, loose now, flowed around her fair oval of face. The slightly puffy lips glistened in the scant moonlight. Fargo noticed how her long, black lashes curved with sensuous grace against her cheeks.

A soft yipping bark sounded nearby.

"Coyotes?" Julius asked nervously.

"Could be, but we're a little far east of their usual range."

"Maybe those Cheyenne? I hear Indians are expert mimics."

"They are," Fargo said, "but so, they say, is Reed McKinney."

"Well, you're the night roundsman now," Julius said, stifling a yawn. "I'm turning in."

Fargo moved onto the crown of the nearest hill for a better view, staying low to avoid skylining himself. The black velvet fabric of night revealed only a few stars, the inky fathoms between them like dark maws opening to devour this puny human. Skeletal cottonwood branches turned the moon into a spiderweb.

More yipping barks, a few deep owl hoots. Fargo took several circular turns around the cold camp. He studied all three horses, especially his Ovaro, but none had caught a danger scent.

A surprise awaited Fargo when he returned to camp. Megan Kinkaid was not only wide awake, but she stood in just her thin muslin chemise, dampening a washcloth from Fargo's canteen.

"Hi," she greeted him. "By necessity, I've learned to bathe with very little water. And I *must* have a bath."

"You little fool," Fargo said without heat. "That's the last of our water. Besides, you ought to be asleep. You have guard next."

Even as he admonished her, however, his eyes, well adjusted to night vision by now, feasted on this vision of female pulchritude. The deeply cut bodice of the chemise showed the tantalizing swells of her breasts, like lush fruits tumbling out of a sack. Fargo felt a warm glow in his groin.

He could hear Julius snoring from his bedroll. But the Trailsman reluctantly reminded himself that he was on guard duty.

Megan, watching him boldly in the luminous moonlight, hitched the chemise over her hips and began cosseting her love nest with slow swirls of the cloth. Watching Fargo watch her, her breathing turned a little ragged.

"Feels good," she taunted him. "Especially when I add images of you replacing the cloth. Is that all right?"

"It's just peachy," he replied, fully aroused. "But not at the moment. You hold those thoughts."

"Hold these," she begged, wantonly pulling the chemise high enough to bare both lovely breasts. "Better yet, play with them."

28

Fargo felt that warm glow turn into a fire at full bellows. Megan's Grand Tetons were works of art, full and supple as if ready to burst with ripeness. The flawless, creamy skin ended in impressive nipples made stiff by night chill and her own busy fingers.

Fargo was almost grateful when the sound of a twig snapping, about fifty feet away, pulled him back to duty.

"Chicken!" she called after him in a whisper. A tinkling laugh followed. "I'm too much woman for the big, bad buckskin man!"

Fargo levered a round into the Henry, listening to the darkness. He sent a quick cross-shoulder glance at Megan. "Pipe down, you jay! I'm trying to listen."

She laughed again, pulling her chemise back down. A heart skip later Fargo froze in midstep when two arms like tree trunks encircled Megan from behind and pulled her into the shadows!

Fargo cursed when he realized his lust had made him fall for the oldest trick in the books, a diversion. Reed McKinney must have snapped that stick while 'Bama Jones snatched Megan.

"Stir your stumps!" Fargo shouted to Julius. "Stay here and shoot anything that moves. I'm going after Megan."

"Going aft—? Where the hell is she?"

Fargo, knees and elbows pumping, ignored the question and raced forward, following the noises of flight. It wasn't his way to charge headlong into the water until he had taken the temperature, but this situation was dangerously different. Fargo had learned, from bad experience, that a woman abducted in the lawless West had better be rescued mighty damn quick or she was a gone-up case.

"Fargo!" called a mocking voice. "Here's something to stay your belly!"

A six-gun opened up, firing so rapidly there was no pause between cartridge detonations. Bullets thrummed past Fargo's head as Reed McKinney fanned the hammer of a Colt Navy, but the Trailsman bore inexorably forward. His enemies had probably already scouted this region, so Fargo's best hope now—*Megan's* best hope—

was to make a fool's dash, consequences be damned. Grifter or not, Megan was a woman. Fargo knew, and lived, the code of this new land—women must be protected at any cost.

Their horses couldn't be too far ahead. Fargo could tell, by the sudden opening up of the sky, that he had left the cover of the sand hills. The terrain now was a swathe of erosion gullies and scattered boulders dividing two flat plains. Low scrub growth threatened to tackle Fargo.

"Take your pills, Fargo!" McKinney's voice brayed before his short iron barked again. Fargo lowered his profile as several slugs whined over him—even shooting in the dark, by ear alone, the bounty hunter was deadly.

A horse whickered, dead ahead, and Fargo felt a new urgency. He bolted even more recklessly forward, his Henry at a high port. Fargo's scouting experience saved him as he adjusted instinctively to any brush or rocks that might trip him.

Now, however, he was getting close, and Reed seemed more determined to plug him. Fargo caught glimpses of orange muzzle flash and knocked the thong off his Colt, spearing it from the holster. Hoping that 'Bama was holding Megan, Fargo opened up a running gun battle with the draw-shoot killer.

Changing tack after every shot, wincing at the close wind-rip of Reed's bullets, Fargo pressed ever forward, determined to rattle his foes and impede their escape with Megan. Reed's guns fell silent, perhaps because he was reloading.

A long, tense, eerie silence settled over everything like a thick quilt. Fargo's acute hearing detected nothing but the bit-champing of still-unseen horses.

Why haven't they escaped yet? Fargo's mind wondered. He supplied his own answer: *because they're waiting to kill you.*

Nonetheless, Fargo decided to roll the bones and keep moving forward. Hesitation in battle, as in love, got a man nowhere. If those two hardcases ever got Megan away from here, her life was forfeit.

Fargo hooked left to approach them from an oblique angle. He was barely under way, walking on his heels now, when the heavy metallic click of a scattergun's hammer being pulled back made a cold fist grip his heart: 'Bama Jones and his smoke pole from hell!

Fargo's bowels felt loose and heavy with fear. When Reed's voice shouted this time, he sounded close enough to touch. "Time to call in the cards, Fargo! Shoot the bastard to dog meat, 'Bama!"

Knowing what was coming, Fargo stretched himself out in a diving leap and barely gained the shelter of a tumble of small boulders before hellfire erupted.

BWAM!

Ear-stinging concussions, one after another, turned the quiet prairie night to bedlam. Pausing only long enough to rotate the next preloaded barrel into place, Jones emptied all five shotgun shells at Fargo. Muzzle flash turned night into day as hundreds (no, thousands, Fargo realized) of pellets ripped everything to doll stuffing all around him. Massive 'Bama was well practiced in controlling the thumping recoil of his destructive weapon.

Fargo, though in mortal danger and scared spitless, had to grudgingly marvel at the brutal power of that heavy, awkward-to-hold weapon. It flayed a scrub pine of its bark, scratched sparks from rocks, and smacked the very atmosphere with its terrible authority. The noise alone could make a stout man whimper, and the bitter stench of spent black powder brought tears to Fargo's eyes.

The men spoke soft and low, but Fargo's hearing was trained by open spaces, and he heard them across the dark divide of night.

"You kill him?"

"Can't tell, hoss. You see anything?"

"Christ. Didja at least hit him?"

"Hard to say."

Fargo laughed silently when Reed—it had to be him asking the questions—cursed like a track-bed laborer. But Fargo's moment of mirth passed instantly as he sized up his situation and realized he had to keep up the strut without hesitating.

"Seize the main chance," he muttered.

At the moment neither of his enemies knew his exact position. However, that could change in a heartbeat, given their savvy trailcraft. Fargo's finger curled around the trigger of his Henry and took up the slack.

Then slackened again as he realized: the point is to surprise, mystify, and confuse your enemies. You want them forced to ignore Megan so you can snatch her back.

Fargo grounded the Henry and reached down to grip the long, narrow Arkansas toothpick in his boot. It slid out as if oiled, and Fargo rose quickly to a crouch, looking up toward the sky until he caught 'Bama's hulking silhouette.

" 'Bama, don't stand their picking your teeth like a soft brain," Reed's voice said in a low whisper. "Get that gun loaded—*Jesus!*"

Fargo's blade chunked somewhere into 'Bama's body and made a sound like a cleaver hacking a side of beef. The bounty hunter roared louder than his big gun. "I'm hit, Reed, the son of a bitch run a frog-sticker into me!"

"Shut up, you damn fool," Reed hissed. "Get your belt gun out—he's still here."

'Bama ignored him and kept howling like a man losing a leg to a rusty saw. "You ain't the one with a knife in you!"

Fargo had crept closer now and could see better. Cursing, Reed grabbed the handle of the Arkansas toothpick and jerked the weapon roughly from 'Bama's right shoulder muscle. 'Bama yelped and began complaining anew. Fargo finally spotted Megan. She was gagged with a bandanna and her wrists and ankles were bound.

Fargo couldn't kill the two men without endangering the woman behind them, so he stuck to his plan. He'd kept the Henry in reserve for this and now drew on its bullet capacity as, aiming high to spare Megan, he squeezed off round after round and kept the bounty hunters off guard for an attack.

Horses reared, one almost bolting. Reed, about to seize Megan, was forced instead to grab the wild-eyed paint's bridle.

A few of Fargo's ricocheting bullets skipped lethally close to Reed. Fargo didn't let him collect his wits, just kept the shots flying.

'Bama, unable to use his right arm, could not swing his formidable bulk into leather.

"Reed!" he begged. "You gotta help me sit my horse!"

Reed cursed a blue streak, using one hand to control his horse and the other to help his partner. The main chance, Fargo decided, had finally arrived. And it wouldn't arrive again.

He dropped the Henry and burst forward, seeing Megan where she stood helpless. She was a handful of feathers to lift and hold, but the three-beat tattoo of galloping hooves retreating didn't mean the fight was over quite yet. Reed's six-gun cracked to life and Fargo felt wind kiss him from the slugs.

"Hold on, Frenchie," Fargo warned. He tossed Megan unceremoniously to the ground and sprawled on top of her, covering her nearly naked body with his.

If she objected, Fargo sure as hell couldn't tell it. He had never been one to link danger and sexual arousal, but she appeared to be the type. She squirmed around until their bodies were locked in a perfect fit. The animal heat from her quickened Fargo's breathing.

Reed's gun fell silent, and Fargo heard their horses retreating farther onto the open plains. He took the gag off Megan. If she had been scared witless by her ordeal, her greeting didn't show it.

"Mr. Fargo, aren't you rather forward? Why, I barely have a stitch on!"

"Faint heart never won fair lady," he informed her, taking possession of those teasing lips.

Mewling with pent-up passion, Megan arched her back so Fargo could slide the chemise up, his hands gliding on satin-smooth skin. Then she pulled his shirt up until the firm points of her breasts were nestled in his chest hair. She ground them into him.

"Fargo! Damn it, Fargo! Is Megan all right?"

Julius's worried voice made both of them reluctantly break from a deep kiss.

"Damn," Fargo said, forced to wait until his voice was steady. Then, "She's safe, Julius! She's with me. But they're still out there. Go back to camp in case they try to flank us."

"Do you really believe that?" she scoffed.

"Your father is the only one who needs to believe it."

By now Megan had reached down to open his fly. When his straining manhood sprang free, hard and insistent, she cooed in delight. "And I teased you about being little? A person could hold a log-rolling contest on this."

"Please do," Fargo invited. He had no idea if the saucy little grifter had ever been taken on the ground before like a wild animal, but she wasn't at all squeamish. She raised her legs and pulled them apart, spreading wide to egg Fargo on.

Fargo lined up perfectly by feel, pausing at the very opening of her womanhood to stroke her pearl with the swollen dome of his shaft. She began to squirm immediately, her sex even more wet and ready. Fargo's hips thrust when he entered and plunged his entire curving length into her.

"Fargo!" she gasped out. "I didn't know it would be like—this, *oh* yes, do that again . . ."

Her talented love muscles worked his member like fingers. The tickling ache, the need for release, seized them together. Fargo, hardly aware himself, had to cover her mouth when she shrieked in the throes of a thrashing climax. Fargo, too, went into the strong finish and gasped at the intensity of his release.

It took Fargo some time before he could move off of Megan and listen to the night again.

"Hope you liked that," she said, her voice kittenish and sleepy. "I certainly did."

"We need to get back to camp," Fargo said.

"Why? Do you really think they'll come back for more this very night? One of them was wounded."

"Nah, they'll likely call it quits for tonight," Fargo agreed. "When I picked up my knife, I found plenty of blood spatters. 'Bama won't die, but he'll be stove up."

"Then why go back to camp just now?" she persisted. "I'll bet you're ready to go again right now. Just like me. Oh, let's do it again. The second time is always the best."

"Fargo!" Julius shouted from camp. "You didn't say *which* flank, damn it! Where are you two?"

Megan groaned but Fargo tugged her to her feet. "*That's* why. We'll have other opportunities."

"We'll *make* other opportunities," she insisted, falling into step behind him.

6

"Christ, Reed, he hit me in the dark! Is Fargo a cat?"

Reed McKinney just about had a belly full of 'Bama's pissing and moaning. The man would face down hot lead, would kill anything you told him to. But he was stupid as a stump, and the man who killed Skye Fargo wouldn't be stupid.

The two men were returning to their crude cold camp east of the sand hills, horses holding a slow trot.

"You're full of sheep dip," Reed snapped, his mouth set like a trap. "Fargo got lucky, that's all. A fish always looks bigger underwater. But he'll be a fish *outta* water when I force his hand in a gunfight."

A coyote yipped, and Reed snapped into the moment. "It's those blasted Cheyenne, springing a trap for us! Raise dust!"

Both riders sank steel into their sore-used mounts, roweling them savagely. Arrows *fwipped* in, narrowly missing them. McKinney and Jones whipped their mounts to the only speed beyond a gallop, the head-long run.

The Cheyenne, in true warrior style, boldly exposed themselves in the dim moonlight, proving to their enemy they weren't afraid. Reed grinned and skinned a Colt. These blanket asses were headed to the happy hunting ground—he could knock the eyes out of a buzzard at two hundred yards.

However, the Indians knew their enemy. Before he could draw a bead, they reverted to the defensive riding style red men had perfected for facing repeating arms on the open plains. They fell to the protected side of the pony's neck, hanging on for dear life and putting their bodies low behind the horse's bulk.

This offered very little human target, so Reed simply shifted beads to their ponies and dropped both. Only the braves' dexterity saved them from injury as they let go and tumbled along the ground.

They reached their camp without further incident, and Reed squatted on his rowels to stir up their old ashes. 'Bama, hissing at the pain, peeled off his shirt to expose the knife wound in his shoulder.

"Where's the rotgut?" Reed demanded.

'Bama pulled a bottle of cheap wagon-yard whiskey from a saddlebag and handed it to his partner. Reed knocked off several slugs and lowered the bottle, wiping his lips on his dirty flannel sleeve.

"Bo," he said as he splashed burning liquor into 'Bama's wound, "might be I called it wrong about one thing. 'Pears Fargo *has* thrown in with the Kinkaids. Prob'ly so's he can get his bell rope pulled by pretty Miss Megan."

"*Christ* that hurts," 'Bama whined.

"Nerve up." Reed ignored him, his chiseled face angry in the moonlight. "I don't favor takin' sloppy seconds. He stole our woman. But with Fargo planted, the other two are ducks on a fence."

'Bama shook his head. "We didn't plant him tonight, did we? Fargo's got no plans to die."

"Quit your white-livered puling," Reed snapped. "There's no gainsaying Fargo's balls. And he's a dead aim with rifle or short gun. But he's a frontiersman, *not* a gunfighter—slapping leather ain't his style. I'll force his hand. And bo, a man don't finish second place in a gunfight. You win or you die."

Fargo woke up the next morning with several problems on his mind, not the least of which was the stolen bank money in his pannier. It was an irritant growing into a tumor.

"We need to kill two birds with one stone," he told Megan and Julius over a meager breakfast of coffee and ash pone. "You two have no supplies and mine are stretched thin. I know of a trading post west of here on the Arkansas River. It's a stop for the express riders, so we can also send the money back to the Grangers Bank in Plum Creek."

"Damn fool notion," Julius grumped. "Megan and I worked hard for that money."

"That's a crock and you know it. If I hadn't been afraid you'd be hanged, Julius, I'd've hauled you both before Sheriff Davis."

"Even me, Skye?" Megan teased, fluttering those long lashes.

"Hardly matters," Julius said smugly. "Skye's one of us now and the sheriff's prime suspect. That's what you get for turning a crime into your own private theater."

"You've struck a lode there," Fargo agreed, scowling. "Let's dust our hocks."

By midmorning the three horsebackers were awash in vast plains undulating all around them like curtain folds. Fargo watched wind move through the grass like waves. Most people, especially women, were horrified by the emptiness of the plains. Fargo, however, considered them a natural wonder of the American West, a perfect symbol of its vast, limitless majesty.

Before long gray sheets of rain came slanting down. The water stung like buckshot when the wind gusts drove it almost horizontally. However, storms out here rarely lasted long. And as soon as it ended, Fargo caught a glimpse of Donaldson's Trading Post on the Arkansas.

Soon Megan and Julius, too, spotted walls of sawed-off cottonwood logs with an iron-reinforced pole gate that stood wide open.

"Who owns it?" Megan asked, holding her broad-brimmed sun hat up to see better.

"A salty old trapper named Elijah Donaldson," Fargo replied, switching his hands on the reins to rest his arms. "He opened it near the end of the fur-trapping era. He realized that his breed had no future once the London dandies grew tired of beaver hats."

"He keep much money around?" Julius asked casually.

Fargo's crisp blue eyes bored into the grifter like augers. "Put it out of your mind right now. If he doesn't shoot you, I will."

By the time they were within hailing distance of the post, the sun blazed with furnace heat and mud daubers were active in the last, rapidly evaporating puddles from the storm.

A gaunt but spry old-timer wearing a beaver hat stepped through the gates to meet them. His voice was like gravel shifting in a bucket. "Fargo, you son of sin, the hell you doin' haulin' them city whippersnappers around? This child is plumb astounded! You got you a powdered wig now, too, and mebbe one a them-air fancy pisspots with paintin' on 'em?"

The old trader had an ugly but affable face distinguished by a snaggle-toothed grin. Julius looked curious, Megan astounded, Fargo amused.

"Skye goldang Fargo! A mild man until pushed and then a hellcat unleashed." Elijah paused, getting a closer look at Fargo's ready-for-battle face. "And I see how some foolish jasper *has* been a-pushin'. Is he buzzard bait yet?"

"Hey up, old roadster," Fargo greeted his friend. "What's on the spit?"

Elijah threw his arms out wide. "This may be a post, but God kiss me if you'll see much trading these days. Most of the pilgrims still hanker for Oregon, not the plains."

Fargo nodded. He had noticed only a few stubborn and isolated homesteaders trying to prove up government land in this rain-scarce grazing country.

Elijah shifted his rheumy old eyes to Julius, dismissed him, and lingered on the supple young woman. He sized her up boldly from her pretty satin shoes to her magnificent silver tiara.

"You mean to leave her here?" he asked Fargo hopefully. "I still got cribs out back left over from when I ran that string of Indian whores. We'll split the money next time you ride in. We'll spit on it now, eh?"

Megan, busy swinging down from her mare with Fargo's help, paled.

Fargo laughed wickedly. "She's not a sporting gal, Elijah, you damn lump of coal. This lady and her father are magicians from New Orleans. Our trails have crossed for a bit."

A copper-tinted mixed-breed boy leaped forward to take the three horses. Fargo watched Julius quickly untie the hidebound bag, again taking great care with it.

"Want me to carry it?" he asked Julius from a deadpan.

"Your skepticism is duly noted," the grifter replied. "What's all the fuss? I told you these are things Megan and I require in our work—things necessary to our survival."

Fargo let it go, watching a contrite Elijah turn toward Megan. "Miss, you are pretty as four aces, and I'm after beggin' your forgiveness. This is woman-scarce country, and most men are glad to marry any female with one jaw tooth left. When I seen your, uh, florid feathers, nat'chally—"

"You're forgiven, Elijah," she said, cutting off his rambling.

Elijah dropped back behind her and winked at Fargo. "I see you're wrinkling the quality linen nowadays, boy."

"Beats Rosy Palm and her four daughters," Fargo told him, winking back. But he hoped he hadn't misstepped in covering for the Kinkaids. Fargo already had bank swag to return and didn't plan to clean up after the grifters here.

Elijah led all three new arrivals to a rain barrel where they rinsed off the trail dust. Then he took them inside the long, low cottonwood building. The plank floor and even the walls were stained by tobacco juice despite the brass spittoons scattered around. War bonnets and rawhide shields adorned the walls.

"I see you're livin' close to that pouch, boy," Elijah told Fargo as they bellied up to a crude plank bar—there were no tables, only additional counters along the side walls. "Hope you ain't countin' on express service?"

"Matter fact I was," Fargo replied. Frustration made his jaw muscles bunch tighter. This was the first time he'd been tempted to throw away money. "No service, I take it?"

"Bring us a bottle of the Bourbon County, Sally," Elijah told the Negro woman behind the bar. "And a glass for the lady."

He looked at Fargo again. "Nothin'. Last riders either

40

killed or quit. Got Comanche raiding this way, plus Southern Cheyenne and Pawnee. And them's just the free-ranging savages. You also got the entire Indian Territory just south of us, and *them* red sons like to go on sprees, too."

"Where's the next place," Fargo asked, "where the express riders still operate?"

Elijah watched the three of them closely while he poured Megan's drink. "Mite queer, a trio like you so desperate for an express rider."

"Anytime you stumble near a point," Fargo invited him, "feel free to make it."

Elijah grinned. "The next place this child knows of is Miller's Bend, due south of here on the Cimarron."

"I've heard of it," Fargo said, watching a man with the look and strong smell of a buffalo hider enter the grog shop and join several others, who were leaning against the side wall and drinking. "I hear it's a lawless hellhole."

"Like most of this territory," Elijah agreed.

"Can one make transportation arrangements there?" Megan asked. "Connections to the east?"

"Got 'em a short-line Overland stage that'll take you to the railroads. But, ma'am, I would advise *no* woman to venture into Miller's Bend, and most especial a young looker like you."

They returned to the trading post. The Trailsman said, "I'll need a hundred-count box of shells for the Henry. Make sure it's factory ammo, not hand-crimped."

Fargo flipped two five-dollar gold pieces onto the deal counter. "This'll cover everything, old-timer."

"You can forget about the Medicine Lodge treaties," Elijah warned Fargo's departing back. "We got warpath Indians on the prowl! Watch your topknot!"

"That old man could use a bath," Megan grumped as Fargo led them south toward the Cimarron, finally breaking a long silence. "Even the horses were curried. Why couldn't *we* bathe, Skye?"

"There's hotels at Miller's Bend with more privacy," he told her, letting the Ovaro get a good smell of the ground. "And an Overland office. You two need to haul your freight back east in a puffin' hurry."

"Why was that old fart deliberately trying to scare us?" Julius asked. "Sure, we had a couple of nasty set-tos with those bounty hunter chaps. But I've seen no sign of them since then. We—"

Fargo raised a hand to silence him. "You've missed all the signs because you won't stop batting your gums. Men who survive out here keep their mouths shut and their eyes open. Look over your right shoulder. See anything?"

Megan, too, looked. "Nothing," they replied together.

"Well, you're both wrong," Fargo informed them. "Dead wrong. Dust puffs have been trailing us for at least two miles. Somebody's coming to kill us."

7

"*Who* is coming to kill us?" Megan demanded. "Those bounty hunters?"

Fargo shrugged a shoulder. "Either them or their hirelings. 'Bama Jones is stove up, and I hear Reed McKinney likes to have Jones backing his play. With Cheyenne breathing down their necks, I think they've hired buffalo hiders to kill me. With me out of the picture, that leaves you two ripe for the plucking."

"What are buffalo hiders like—as enemies, I mean," Julius asked.

"Generally they're poor shakes as fighters. Weak discipline and they put their own survival above the group's. But this brand of hider also does his own hunting—their one skill is scoring hits at long range. They do it for a living."

Fargo sent a long, searching glance over his shoulder, eyes slitted in the strong afternoon light.

"They use the big-bore smoke wagons," he resumed. "Weapons that can drop a bull buffalo from a mile off. The Big Fifty Sharps and Hawken guns like Elijah's. Hand cannons."

Julius and his daughter exchanged tight-lipped glances.

"How long," Julius asked, "before we reach Miller's Bend?"

"Not quite two days," Fargo replied. "Or maybe never if you don't stop pulling your horse's nose up. Let him smell new ground and he'll settle down."

"Are they still behind us?" Megan asked.

Fargo nodded, half his bearded face in shadow under his hat. " 'Bout six or seven riders."

"Are they getting closer?"

"Nah. They don't need to. They're plainsmen; they're just waiting for the earth to curve in their favor. Then they'll set up crossed sticks and open fire on me."

"Why don't we just outrun them?" Megan urged. "We have good horses, freshly grained and watered. Some of these men, I noticed back at the trading post, are riding old mules."

"We could rabbit," Fargo agreed. "But trouble never goes away on its own if you run from it. Either we take it by the horns or we suffer a hard goring."

"Spoken like a rustic hero," Julius said, scorn poison-tipping his words. "Say, what about those two Indians? Any sign of them?"

"Haven't actually seen them," Fargo replied. "But this morning they sent up smoke, and it's heap big doin's. I can't read it, though. Each tribe protects its code."

A few seconds later the first spiraling plume of dust kicked up on Fargo's right, followed by a reverberating bellow as the sound of the gunshot caught up. The Ovaro twitched but held his pace.

"They don't want you two," Fargo reminded them. "But accidents happen. Just remember not to ride in a straight line for too long, or else they'll lead on us and find their range."

Another round came thumping in, and Julius nervously took the .38 Smith & Wesson from his waistband. Fargo watched him swing the wheel out to check his loads. The chamber under the hammer was empty.

"That's hogwash about leaving your hammer on an empty chamber," Fargo told him. "You'll need every bullet in a scrape."

"My thoughts precisely," the grifter said, thumbing in the sixth round.

The next bullet hummed dangerously close past Fargo's left ear, and this time he rode into action. He reined the Ovaro sharply around and ki-yied him up to a gallop, going on the attack.

Fargo speared the freshly oiled Henry from its saddle sheath and jacked a round into the chamber. He knew that few ambushers ever expected their quarry to charge them, and he counted on the element of surprise to rattle them as he thundered closer.

The Trailsman could not hope to match the range of his opponents' buffalo guns with a Henry, nor their knockdown power. The smaller-caliber Henry did, however, have the advantage of speed of operation and superior magazine capacity. Fargo put both to good use as he raced over the plain.

Several hiders had already panicked and were in retreat. A few more, however, stubbornly held their prone positions and kept firing. Fargo knew they were sighting on the Ovaro's massive chest, and he fought like a demon to keep their aim off course. His bullets peppered their positions with increasing accuracy.

A buff gun straight ahead of him belched blue smoke, but Fargo had jerked the reins hard left just before the lethal, half-ounce buffalo ball could rip the stuffings out of his horse. He stood up in the stirrups, howling like a madman as he levered the Henry without pause.

That tore it. The last hiders bolted for their mounts, some deserting their guns. Fargo was not bloodthirsty, and although he was within his rights to shoot them as they fled, repugnance for back-shooting stayed his hand. He rode ahead to join his two companions.

"Did you kill anyone just now?" Megan asked.

Fargo shook his head. "Didn't need to. But that will change. Reed and 'Bama are behind this, and they need you two or your heads to prove they caught you. And nothing's going to stop them but a bullet."

Custom dictated that Indian warriors never broach an important subject too directly. Plenty Coups and Shoots Left-handed smoked for some time and discussed inconsequential matters. Finally, having smoked to the Four Directions, they laid the pipe down between them. Now the serious talk could begin.

"It is as clear as a blood spoor in new snow," Shoots Left-handed told his battle companion. Their scarred chests and arms, pocked by burns and old bullet wounds, told the violent history of their life in the West. "The butchers mean to kill Son of Light. And you cannot step on the tail of a rattler unless you expect it to strike back."

Plenty Coups, his feet aching like his companion's, nodded. "These are words I can pick up and place in my parfleche, buck. You saw him again just now, this warrior! The man whites call the Trailsman may kill the butchers before we can. If this happens, the arrows will never be renewed."

The two braves crouched in a grassy swale well south of the sand hills where their horses had been slain. Though horse tribesmen now, the Cheyenne people had fought for centuries as foot warriors. Stuffing their moccasins with dried grass to soften the sharp edges of stones, Shoots Left-handed and Plenty Coups had trailed their enemies on foot. From this rear position, they saw the two *mah-ish-ta-shee-da* devils look on as the hiders were routed by Son of Light.

"We must have ponies," Shoots Left-handed said. "True, we have kept pace so far. But on foot we will stay too hungry and exhausted to fight."

"Chief Yellow Bear saw our smoke," Plenty Coups said confidently. "He is Lakota, his daughter married into my clan. His camp is close by on Weeping Woman Creek. We will have new ponies."

"We were fools," Shoots Left-handed said, "to think these white butchers would take the fight to us and not our horses. I believed that manly pride would make them want to defeat us fairly."

"Pride?" Plenty Coups repeated. "Go ask your mother for a dug! Pride is as foreign to them as honor. To them, even children and the unborn in the womb are not innocent. They kill everything, and there is no importance in the killing."

"As you say." The furrow between Shoots Left-handed's eyes deepened in a frown as he watched the two white devils. "They stand too far distant for us to kill without horses. No pride, no honor, their very presence destroys the red man. The fierce Blackfeet to the north wiped out by the white man's yellow vomit, the entire Crow Nation unmanned by their strong water. *These* two, at least, will be ours."

"Your thoughts roam with mine," Plenty Coups said.

"But events may defeat our plans. The butchers lust for this woman. If they kill Son of Light, so be it. But if he kills them, you know our world becomes a hurting place. We must get ponies and return to the fight. We will kill the two devils only, but if Son of Light tries to count first coup on them, he too is marked for death. We must do it for the People."

"Jesus Katy Christ," Reed McKinney said, disgust twisting his cruel mouth. "A blind whore with a squirrel gun coulda put on a better show than that one."

'Bama didn't hear a word Reed said. "My damn shoulder is stiff," he complained as the two men walked slowly toward a greasy form crumpled in the grass. "Sumbitch is really givin' me gyp, Reed. Sorter burnin' and itchin' like. That damn frog-sticker of Fargo's—"

"Help me!" begged the man on the ground. He was one of the seven hiders who tried to kill Fargo—the so-called leader of the bunch. Reed had watched his horse throw him during the rout by Fargo. One glance told the bounty hunter it was curtains for the man—his spine was broken.

"Please help me," the hider begged. "Can't move my legs."

"Sure. That's only Christian." Reed pulled the single-edged bowie from his sash and knelt beside the injured man. "Lots of pain, huh?"

"Savage pain. Huh-hurts every place."

Reed's face turned dark and ugly. "So you're all grit and a yard wide, huh? Good thing I didn't pay you in advance. You weak-sister son of a bitch, you make me wanna puke."

"*Gut* the gal-boy, Reed!" 'Bama exclaimed, caught up in the thrill of senseless homicide. "And once it's in him, give it the Spanish twist!"

The man's wrenching scream when the bowie opened him up from navel to crotch startled even 'Bama into respectful attention. Reed rough-gutted him like game shot along the trail.

He wiped his blade clean in the grass and stood up to look at 'Bama. "I see now it's buildin' up to Fargo and me, eyeball to eyeball. Let's fork leather and pay him a visit."

8

Only a few hours of light remained, but Fargo had no intention of letting the grass grow under them. This father-daughter confidence team spelled bad trouble, and he wanted them off his hands as soon as possible. Worse, he was in possession of stolen loot. He wouldn't breathe easy until it was tucked into the mail pouch on an express rider's horse.

The country hereabouts was rolling plains, high elevation with thinner air that forced the horses to blow more frequently. Now and then Fargo slewed around in the saddle to check their backtrail. He spotted nothing but knew the killers were back there—probably waiting for nightfall when their quarry would camp.

"If these two bounty hunters are so tough," Megan said, "why did they hire those hiders to try and kill you?"

Julius spoke up quickly. "Haven't you figured that out yet, child? Mr. Fargo has earned himself a reputation, one that was carved out beyond the fringes of civilization. These two men are leery to test it."

"No, I think I've puzzled out the real reason," Fargo replied. "It's those two Cheyenne trailing them. They've put up a vengeance pole and now they have to either kill the bounty hunters or die trying. McKinney and Jones are taking them seriously—they can't come after us while Cheyenne braves stalk them."

"I'm rooting for the Cheyenne," Julius said. "But where are they?"

"That's got me treed, too," Fargo admitted. "I hate to say it, but I think they're gone."

"As in . . . dead?" Megan asked.

Fargo tilted his hat to counter the westering sun. "Could be. Let's hope not. That deals the two jackals a stronger hand."

Fargo raised one arm and placed his hand between the sun and the horizon: four fingers left, about thirty minutes of sunlight. The sky was cloudless, meaning plenty of starlight, and he considered simply riding all night. After all, they were in open plains with few rocks or holes to lame a horse, especially at a trot.

However, he decided against it. While not exhausted, the horses had been holding a steady gait. They needed to rest and graze. Even as he debated all this, they crested a low hill and spotted a rain-sheltered covert. A backwater of the Cimarron formed its southern border, with hock-high bunchgrass already making the horses fight their bits.

"It's *too* perfect a campsite," Fargo mused. "McKinney and Jones have worked the Kansas Territory since it opened, covered all of it. They'd know about this place. Even so, let's take the bait. Best way to cure a boil is to lance it. Besides, the horses will rebel if we push on."

Fargo swung down and stepped over to help Megan down. His hand took some liberties, and she blew him a kiss.

"Christ!" Julius said, watching his daughter with a look of disgust. "Why don't you two just copulate in the saddle? I'll go invite those Indians to watch."

"You ever notice, Skye," Megan said, "how it's always the men without women who harangue the pleasures of the marital bed?"

"Marital? All you know about him is his name."

"Daddy dear just needs someone to wrap his leg around at night."

"You scandalous, immoral woman!" Julius protested, his cultured face now twisted with rage.

"Here, don't drop those reins," Fargo protested sharply as Julius abandoned his horse and started toward his daughter. "You know horses piss in the same water they drink. What you two drink is your bee's wax, but you *will* hold back those horses until I drink."

"Sorry," Julius said, taking the reins from Fargo.

Fargo drank, filled his canteen, and let the Ovaro drink. Then he took a good look around in the rapidly dying light. All three travelers had their loaded weapons in hand.

"Let's give our friends out there a picture of domestic bliss to chew on," Fargo called to his companions.

He sighted the Henry on a rabbit, in the last light of day, and popped it over, dead after a few fast twitches. With no apparent concern for enemies, he skinned it with his Arkansas toothpick, spitted it with a green stick, and placed it over a driftwood fire to cook.

"Mr. Fargo, we have ample provisions," Julius pointed out. "Killers are out there. What is the point of all this?"

"Hot meat beats hardtack and salt pork. And the *point* is to keep our enemy surprised, confused, and mystified. They don't expect this right now."

"How about guard duty tonight?" Megan asked. "Will I have a shift?"

Fargo trusted her alert senses. "Why not? We won't be leaving the camp area, so the sentry is really in no more danger than the other two. Keep your mind focused—"

"—on the here and now," she finished for him.

"Yeah. Your dad first, then you, then me."

She brightened. Keeping her voice low she said, "How about after you relieve me you *relieve* me?"

"If I was ever tempted . . . but that's exactly when they'll strike. We'll have to hold off a bit."

Fargo had already tethered the Ovaro in the grass with Megan's chestnut and Julius's palomino. Under a starshot sky and a pale half moon he walked concentric circles around the camp, the Henry in his left hand, his right palming the butt of his Colt.

An owl hooted, and Fargo thought about Reed McKinney.

He returned to camp and accepted a hunk of rabbit and a cup of coffee from Megan.

He ate, then announced, "I'm turning in. Heads up on guard duty."

Despite feeling bone weary, Fargo lay awake in his blanket. He listened to the endless crackle of insects, the bubbling chuckle of the backwater stream, the soft song of the prairie wind.

Other sounds, too, reached his ears and were instantly classified as harmless or dangerous. The occasional whispering, between father and daughter, Fargo wasn't sure how to classify, given their trade. But the faint clinking of bit rings, a sound so dim it could have been a memory echo, instantly signaled danger.

There was dew in the mornings now, and Fargo was sleeping with his weapons in the blanket to protect them. He stood up, strapped on his Colt, and gripped the Henry in his left hand.

"Why are you stirring?" Julius asked. "I have first watch."

"I have better ears," Fargo retorted. "There's riders out there somewhere."

Fargo moved on out of the covert, following their backtrail. He stayed low to the ground, moving only after listening a long time. Placing his ear just above the ground he thought he detected a hoof pawing the prairie soil.

He went down even lower. Keeping his vision narrow and just off the ground, he discovered what might be the shape of human legs.

They've left their horses, Fargo guessed.

Instinct told him to stop them now, not in camp. Fargo sprawled out in a prone position and opened fire on the leg shapes. The Henry kicked into his shoulder over and over as he sprayed lead, staining the air with the bitter stench of spent powder.

His hunch panned out: horses whickered in fright, men cursed, and a beehive of angry bullets pelted at him. When 'Bama opened up with his mob gun, Fargo ate dirt trying to make himself invisible. Giant fists of dirt were loosened as the multiple-shot scattergun dug tunnels inches from Fargo's head.

The moment the last blast fell silent, however, Fargo sprang up and emptied the rest of the Henry's magazine. He heard them retreat at a gallop.

"Are you all right?" Megan asked him anxiously when Fargo returned and began reloading. "My God, that weapon booms like a cannon."

"My ears are still ringing from it," Fargo said. "But I think I drove them off for the rest of the night."

"You sure about that?" Julius asked with a nervous edge to his tone.

"No," Fargo admitted, crawling into his blanket. "But I'm going to get some sleep anyway. You two keep eyes and ears to all sides."

For hours Fargo napped and woke, grabbing rest in rough handfuls. Several times, at the sound of an owl hooting or a horse stamping, he started awake, his face rigid with the focus of combat.

Each time, the camp was quiet and his trusty Ovaro resting. Fargo dozed off again and took the guard from Megan around three a.m. It was in the still, sleepy darkness just before dawn when the bottom suddenly dropped out of the world.

Fargo had felt trouble coming for some time. Even as he yawned himself awake and thumbed rough crumbs of sleep from his eyes, he noticed that all three horses were alert and pointed toward the south, ears pricked. However, it wasn't the usual trouble alert.

On a hunch, Fargo had placed three fingertips lightly on the ground. Sure enough, it was vibrating from the motion of many unshod hooves.

"Buffalo," Fargo whispered. By this time the great herds of the mountain-man era had been thinned out and broken up by the professional hunters and hiders. But plenty of the shaggy beasts remained.

Fargo wasn't too worried about being stampeded. Bison naturally ran toward open stretches and avoided places that interrupted open space, such as this covert surrounded by trees.

"Skye, you awake?" Megan's sleepy voice whispered from the darkness.

"Wha'd'ya think, girl? I'd sleep on guard?"

"Skye, about that money in the pouch?"

"The *bank* money. What about it?"

"Well . . . thanks to my bungling father, I've lost most of my clothing. There'll likely be a clothing store in Miller's Bend. Couldn't we pinch just a *little* of the—"

"No," Fargo cut her off. "It's not ours to spend. I've got some money. Maybe I can help you out."

"Don't worry, Fargo," Julius's wide-awake voice spoke up in the darkness. "If she needs gloves, she'll just crawl in your bedroll."

"You son of a bitch!" Megan bit off, and Fargo heard her scrambling out of her bedroll, ready to thump on her old man.

"Both of you listen!" Fargo barked in a voice of total command. "Never mind the family feud for now. We've got running buffaloes bearing down on us."

When Fargo again felt the ground, however, he wasn't so sure. The vibrations were lighter than he expected, and the motion he sensed was faster than the long, lumbering gallop of buffalo.

The chestnut and the palomino began rearing on their hind legs, whickering piteously. Their eyes rolled back in response to a primitive call.

"Oh, hell," he whispered, hurrying toward the horses. "I called it wrong." He raised his voice and snapped at the other two: "Quick, double tether your horses, then hobble 'em!"

"But I don't hear any buffaloes," Megan objected as she hurried to catch up.

"It's a *manada* of wild horses," Fargo told her. "That's a master stallion and his scores of mares, with colts and a few weaker stallions tagging along. Feels like hundreds in this *manada*."

Julius joined them as they tied rawhide hobbles on their horses. "But surely they won't attack us? They're horses."

"They'll attack," Fargo assured him, "because they *are* horses—free horses. Some wild stallions are man killers. You can bet they intend to liberate our horses. Mustangs steal saddle-broken horses all the time. If our mounts break free, they *will* join the *manada*."

"I hear them!" Megan exclaimed.

"All right," Fargo said. "Move back into the trees. If you have to, fire your weapons. But only to scare the mustangs."

"Talk about your first-rate con jobs," Julius grumped. "Attack horses! It's a few buffalo, and he's having us on, Megan. That's a favorite sport out west."

"Well, *some*thing's coming!" she cried. "The sound is so loud I can't think!"

"Backs to a solid tree," Fargo ordered. "Here they come!"

A boiling swirl of dust rose up, and Fargo felt the ground vibrating through his soles. The thunder of hooves was punctuated by fierce, high-pitched whinnying. Suddenly the *manada* was on them like a flash flood, swarming around the three horses tethered near the water. Pintos, solid blacks and whites and bays, duns, *grullas* or blues, dapples, every color and marking of horses came in.

"Holy mother of God!" Julius exclaimed. "Look at them!"

The sun hadn't risen yet, but plenty of grainy light revealed the wild horses. Their uncut tails dragged along the ground, and their manes were so long the horses had to constantly toss their heads to free their vision.

The master stallion, a powerful claybank, whinnied fervently at the three tethered animals, encouraging them to run. The Ovaro, along with the Kinkaids' mounts, strained mightily to answer the summons of the wild.

" 'Bama!" shouted a panicked voice somewhere off to Fargo's left. "Where's our horses, you soft-brained fool? I told you to hold them!"

Even as Reed McKinney's voice fell silent Fargo caught a welcome sight: two of the horses forming a mill around the three tethered mounts wore saddles!

Fargo burst out laughing. Leveling his Henry over the horses, he fired several shots. They immediately dashed off to the north, following the master stallion—the bounty hunters' horses and tack with them.

Fargo glanced east. The newborn sun was balanced like a brass coin just above the flat horizon.

"Let's break camp right now," he told his still-stunned companions. "With luck we'll get a good jump on those two buzzards before they steal more horses. And naturally *our* horses are first on their list."

9

Thanks to the charge of the wild horses, Fargo and the Kinkaids had an uneventful journey to Miller's Bend. They rode along the banks of the Cimarron for another full day, made a second camp on a High Plains plateau, and reached Miller's Bend around noon the next day.

"Eureka!" Julius exclaimed when the trio of horse-backers halted on a low bluff overlooking the town. "Megan, we've struck a lode."

More and more emigrants leaving from Saint Joe's and Independence, hearing about the impending Homestead Act, were deciding to settle in the Kansas Territory. The westering fever was still at high pitch, and Miller's Bend fairly hummed with capitalism. Solid lumber buildings alternated with tents and sheds. Vendors with wooden pushcarts hawked honeycombs, sacks of ginger snaps, and buffalo tongues pickled in brine.

"Nix on that 'struck a lode' hogwash," Fargo told Julius. "First thing you do is book passage east. Those two killers won't lag."

"Fargo, stage fare is expensive. And meals at the way stations cost a dollar apiece."

Fargo scowled, having already thought about that. "Just before I had the sweet luck of meeting you two I drew my pay for scouting a wagon train through to the Oregon Territory. Since I'm partly to blame for this damn mare's nest, I'll post the pony." Fargo hooked a thumb over his shoulder. "Have you noticed who's back?"

Megan paled, thinking he meant the bounty hunters.

But it was the two Cheyenne braves, staying well back from the town.

"Why are they following us?" she lamented.

"They aren't. It's McKinney and Jones they want, but they lost that trail when the bounty hunters' horses were shanghaied by the mustangs. So the Indians are sticking close to us knowing we're the lure for McKinney and his half-wit partner."

"Then why did they disappear for a couple days?" Julius wondered.

"I think I figured it out," Fargo said. "They're riding different horses now. I suspect that trick shooter Reed McKinney killed their mounts when they attacked him."

By now they had ridden down onto the main street, and Fargo didn't like it at all. The place had the feel of an end-of-the-track hovel, rough and wide open. Plenty of toughs, many heavily armed and no doubt on the prod, swaggered it around everywhere.

However, the town did have a new hotel and an Overland Stage and Freight office, which also meant a few fashionable ladies in bustles, boas, and pinned-up petticoats. A young woman in a whalebone crinoline stepped down from a six-horse coach.

"Tilting hoops, gents!" a man cried out, and the lounging men enjoyed an illicit glimpse of pantalooned ankle.

"There's the express office," Julius said, his tone goading. "I guess you'll want to send that money back right away?"

"Matter fact," Fargo said, reining in at the tie-rail. "And you're going to witness it."

Despite the seedy town, Fargo trusted the express service throughout the West. The service was expensive, but receipts were given for money and the amount guaranteed by the company. He would also have a legal record that the money was sent to the bank.

"I'll be damned," Julius said when the transaction was complete and they left the office. "I apologize, Fargo. You really are an honest man, aren't you?"

"An honest pagan," he corrected, catching Megan's eye.

The livery stable wasn't far from the hotel, so they rode there first, forced to a slow pace by the chaos and traffic.

"Hep! Hep!" shouted a teamster, cracking his long buckskin lash and guiding his overloaded freight wagon around a drunk who lay sprawled in the street. Six-foot-high wheels and one-inch-thick iron tires dug permanent ruts. Staggering men relieved themselves openly in the street.

"Real family town," Fargo remarked. "And you two stick out like Kansas City fire engines."

Hardcases lounged everywhere, watching the new arrivals from hooded eyes. Two hard-bitten, dirty, bearded riders wearing butternut-dyed cloth trotted past Fargo and company on gaunt mules. Their greasy flap hats were burned and stained from doubling as pot holders.

"The mudsills in this berg are just common riffraff," Julius scoffed.

"No, plenty of them are experienced killers," Fargo warned him. "Jayhawkers and Border Ruffians, private armies that roam the territory. This area is infested with 'em."

The Ute had a saying that nagged at Fargo: *Place no foot down until there is a rock to bear it.* A town, too, needed proper scouting, but once again Fargo was galloping blind into danger.

They turned in at the livery. Fargo paid for rubdowns, a feed, and a night's boarding for all the horses, watching his money pouch go flatter. Out of boredom and curiosity, he had made the stupid decision to watch the Kinkaids swindle a bank manager. Now he was going to pay for it in spades.

"Next stop, the hotel," Megan said, heading along the boardwalk, bustle rustling, toward a five-story frame building, with fancy gold scrollwork over the double doors announcing: THE CIMARRON HOUSE.

" 'Fraid that won't be the next stop," Fargo muttered. "Here's our first badge-toter."

The lawman had stopped ahead of them on the boardwalk, legs spread wide to block the way. Fargo wasn't fooled by the smile and made sure the starman saw him knock the riding thong off the hammer of his Colt.

"Skye Fargo," the law dog greeted him. "Accompanied by Julius Kinkaid and his stunning daughter Megan."

"You have the advantage over us, Sheriff . . . ?"

"Brubaker. Lonny Brubaker. Though I confess I ain't much of a sheriff. Laziness has turned me into a town dough belly. I spend most of my time collecting taxes for the county, a *small cut* going my way."

Brubaker's amiable tone, and his emphasized words, made it clear he was inviting a bribe. He was indeed soft around the middle, but Fargo realized that didn't mean he was weak.

"How long you plan to be here?" Brubaker asked.

"That's no say-so of yours unless we break the law."

"Everything in Miller's Bend is my say-so. Far as breaking the law," he added, "you've done that already. All three of you are wanted. I got a telegram about it. But, see, if I arrest you, that's just doing my job and there's no reward. Maybe there's some other way to arrange this?"

"You're bleeding a turnip, Sheriff," Fargo said. "All three of us are light in the pockets. If we pooled our money we couldn't buy a busted trace chain."

"I doubt that, Fargo. Hell, I myself would pay fifty dollars just to suck on that woman's—"

"Shut your *filthy* sewer!" Megan had the Colt out of her bodice in an eyeblink.

"Easy, hon," Fargo soothed. "He gets a chance to apologize before you kill him."

Brubaker's Adam's apple bobbed hard when he swallowed. The muzzle was pointed at his family jewels.

"Sheriff, a woman may kill for cause when abused as you just abused me," Megan informed him. "No jury would convict me. Now apologize or I will end your line."

"Jesus Christ, honey, I apologize! I'll stick to business. Now, Fargo, no way in hell you three spent that bank money out there in the empty plains. It ain't a king's ransom, but then I ain't royalty. Just plank down the cash and I ignore all of you."

Fargo had no intention of endangering the express rider by saying where the money was. "The money belongs to the people of Plum Creek," he replied.

"Well, no shit. That was also true when you three stole it from 'em."

"I won't pay bribes with it," Fargo clarified. "This little visit has gone about as far as it can go, Sheriff. You'll notice we're all heeled and we intend to stay that way. Nickel-chasers will pay dearly."

Brubaker shrugged. "It's your funeral."

Fargo took each of the Kinkaids by an elbow and guided them around the lawman.

"You got *into* town," he called after them, "but you won't get out without my say-so. That includes by stagecoach. *I* may be soft, Fargo, but not the people I hire."

Rooms at the Cimarron House were an exorbitant five dollars apiece. A cash-strapped Fargo booked a room with double beds, then paid an extra dollar to have a couch dragged in.

"I'll sleep on the couch," he volunteered on their way up to the third floor. "For me that's luxury."

Fargo unlocked the door to their room and looked askance at the canopied beds and gilt mirrors. Gas lamps with crystal-clear globes adorned each wall, mounted in elegant brass sconces shaped like figures from ancient myth. "So this is what I'm paying for?"

Megan laughed. "Skye, you sleep on the ground too much. *This* is how to live."

She unfastened her bustle and clucked in distress as she examined it. She tugged a braided pull rope near the bed, summoning a young porter dressed in red livery.

"Please give this a good dusting," she told him. "And we'll all be needing hot baths."

The porter goggled at the curvaceous beauty. "Yes, ma'am. The maid will be in with hot water and towels."

"Before that bath I'm going to take a squint around," Fargo said. "It won't take our bounty-hunter friends long to get here. Besides, I need to see what kind of plug-uglies are working for Brubaker."

Julius slapped bay rum tonic on his face and grabbed his bowler. "Megan will bathe first, anyway. I think I'll—"

"You and Megan stay right here, understand? Take your baths, but keep the door locked and a chair wedged under it. Keep your weapons handy."

"Well, you're the boss," Julius gave in.

That meek surrender bothered Fargo—it wasn't Kinkaid's way to defer to authority. However, Fargo put it out of his thoughts as he descended into the bustling hotel lobby.

A barroom called the Big Elephant opened off one side of the lobby. Fargo pushed open the slatted batwings and immediately felt tension in the air. A long bar filled the far side wall, with a scattering of green baize card tables occupying the floor. And leaning against the bar, watching Fargo while cleaning his fingernails with a match, was certain trouble.

The thug wore a deputy's badge pinned to a rawhide vest. He was large and barrel-chested and displayed the perpetual sneer of a barracks-room bully. Eyes like hard black agates followed Fargo as he strode over to the bar, ignoring the bully-boy lawman.

"Spot of the giant killer, mister?" asked a barkeep in sleeve garters and a string tie.

"Beer," Fargo said regretfully, for it was only ten cents instead of the two bits for whiskey.

Fargo had already spotted Sheriff Lonny Brubaker. The pudgy lawman sat at a card table with two men, mulling his cards as if they had betrayed him. His nonchalant manner, however, didn't fool the Trailsman. He wasn't here to play cards but to ride herd on his human bonanza.

Fargo sipped his beer and waited for the inevitable trouble. It wasn't long in coming. From the corner of his eye Fargo saw the deputy push away from the bar and move into the space beside him.

"How do you like the Big Elephant?" the deputy greeted him.

Fargo glanced over at him. Lumps of old scar tissue around the man's eyes betokened plenty of bare-knuckle brawling. Brubaker was right—his dirt-workers weren't soft.

"Seems all right," Fargo replied. "Beer's warm, but it's not ice season yet."

"Got us several lively spots in Miller's Bend," the deputy volunteered. He added with a cocky grin, "Got us a real quiet bone orchard, too."

"Which I'm about to plant you in, you pile of human compost," Fargo retorted calmly before he drained his glass.

The remark, spoken with lethal calmness, rocked the deputy back on his heels. Fargo watched his smug grin melt like a snowflake on a river.

"Mister, did I hear you right?"

"It's past discussion," Fargo told him. "You came over here to brace me. So shuck out that hogleg and let's get smokin'."

The deputy sent an uncertain glance toward his boss, who ignored him like a trained actor.

"You get out of here, you son of a bitch! That's a lawful order."

"Here," asked Fargo, meaning the barroom, "or the whole town?"

"The town!"

Fargo shook his head. "That I won't do. You've got no charge against me. Even if you have, it's false."

A large vein began to throb over the deputy's temple. Everyone was watching him, and he was aware of that. "You bolted to the floor, drifter? I said, light a shuck outta Miller's Bend."

Despite the order Fargo knew the deputy's real intent was to kill him. The tin star's right hand twitched closer to his Volcanic as he moved to block Fargo's path. Fargo turned sideways to narrow his target.

"Ease off," Fargo said. "I don't like being close-herded."

That right hand twitched onto the butt of the Smith & Wesson, and Fargo evaluated things quickly. Gunplay in here, especially if it killed a deputy, would force even a crooked sheriff to do his duty. Fargo knew he and the Kinkaids would face rough justice. Better to handle this a different way.

The deputy's hand wrapped the grips, and Fargo stepped intimately close, his left arm blocking the draw. Fargo drew his Colt and savagely buffaloed the man, cracking him across his right temple. The seven-and-a-half-inch barrel scored an instant knockout, the deputy hitting the sawdust-covered floor with a sound like sacked salt hitting hardpan.

Fargo hated using the buffalo maneuver for fear of damaging a weapon, but it was handy if a man wanted to avoid a big stirring and to do. And perhaps he had succeeded—no one seemed particularly worried about the deputy.

On his way out Fargo glanced at Brubaker's table. The grinning sheriff lifted his glass in toast.

"That deputy's a mite unfriendly," Fargo said.

"The hell you expect, a sugar tit? You're an owlhoot now, Fargo, not a hero. I see why you have a reputation, Trailsman. But remember—you just got here."

Fargo made a quick trip to the stage depot and returned to the hotel. He was surprised to find both Kinkaids in the room, and not at each other's throats. His bath was no longer warm, but Fargo scrubbed up anyway, a weapon near each hand and his Arkansas toothpick in the water with him.

"Well, that crooked starpacker wasn't bluffing," Fargo called from behind a three-panel screen, washing his back with a wooden scrubber. "The stage line has been forced to blackball you two by order of the sheriff. So I suggest we just cut our losses and leave. If we have to, we'll ride to Kansas City and put you on a train."

"Leave when?" Megan demanded. "Surely you don't mean now?"

"*Right* now would be too obvious," Fargo told her. "Best time is late tonight, after midnight. I'll know better after I've had a look around the town. There's side streets that need checking, and likely ambush points."

"Midnight!" Megan protested. "We have the room until tomorrow morning, and big, soft beds. *Beds*, Skye! I was hoping we—"

She blushed and fell silent, remembering her father.

"You two better *not* sate your disgusting lust in my proximity," Julius huffed.

"Disgusting? Pater, you need to get your ashes hauled."

Fargo dried off, put on his spare set of buckskins, and pulled Megan's horn comb through his hair.

"Skye, I have to go *some*where," Megan supplicated. "Can't I go look for that dress?"

He buckled on his gun belt. "Sorry, but it's too dangerous. You two are obviously worth good bounties, and I supposedly have nine hundred in bank swag. These are hard times, and that money could tide a man for years. Right now it's not just McKinney and Jones—it's any man who sees the opportunity."

"Well, if you aren't back soon, can we at least go down to the hotel dining room? Meals come with the room fare."

Fargo relented at sight of those fluttering lashes. "All right, *just* the dining room. And keep your weapons close."

Fargo went down into the afternoon sunshine and bustle of Main Street. Miller's Bend did a lively lumber trade, and Fargo could see two gristmills. However, the town was located just across the river from the Indian Territory, and everyone—even a few females—carried arms. This forced Fargo to constant vigilance, alert for the ever-expected attack.

He walked both sides of Main and the two cross streets, making a mental map for tonight's escape—which might even become a lead social if they were caught. Fargo was coming back down Main Street when he realized a familiar-looking figure had stayed behind him too long.

He turned around, right hand palming the butt of his Colt. A gimlet-eyed man with a hard, sneering mouth watched him from a gunfighter's crouch. His .36 Colt Navy revolvers were tied down low in rawhide holsters.

"Reed McKinney," Fargo said. "Didn't take you long to steal more horses."

"Not with a little six-gun persuasion. Long as you're stroking that Sam Colt, why not jerk it?"

"I don't let shitheels goad me into starting a fight. It'll come out when I make the call. Where's your stupid sidekick?"

Reed laughed. "I'll just let you keep wondering about that. He could have the drop on you right now."

Maybe so, but Fargo had no plans to take his eyes off McKinney's hands.

"You took a good chunk outta his shoulder with that toothpick of yours," Reed said. "I wonder how you'd fare against this?"

He stroked the bowie knife in his sash.

"If you're so curious," Fargo invited, "bridge the gap."

A smile twisted Reed's thin, cruelly expressive lips. "Nope. If I kill you here, I'll have to pay tribute money to Lonny Brubaker. Fargo, why'n'cha play this smart? Give me and 'Bama the Kinkaids and you can keep the bank money. Hell, why should we scrap?"

"I got nothing against honest bounty hunters," Fargo said. "But neither one of the Kinkaids will make it back alive. And Megan Kinkaid will be repeatedly raped before you kill her."

"So? I'll bet you're tapping into that stuff."

"No deal," Fargo said.

"So you *are* poking her," McKinney growled. "It's best to check the brand before you drive another man's stock."

"That woman is a free-range maverick. And just a personal word to you—when you hired those stinking hiders to snuff my wick, you made a big mistake. When the time and place are right we *will* be hugging."

The bounty hunter's eyes went smoky with rage. "You sanctimonious asshole, don't you realize it's the dirt nap for you if you keep helpin' them two? Hell, you're sided by a woman and a perfumed barber's clerk in a bowler. Even if you get out of Miller's Bend, which don't hardly seem likely, you got me and 'Bama dogging you. Hand the Kinkaids over, Fargo, and live to bounce your grandkids on your knee."

"No deal," Fargo repeated, turning back around. "Now I'm off like a dirty shirt."

"Fargo! Fargo, you son of a bitch! Stop or I'll burn you down right now!"

If McKinney had meant to kill him, Fargo figured he would have tried by now. But as he sauntered away, he could feel the cold-blooded murderer dividing his back into kill zones. And he wondered, all over again, just how he and the Kinkaids would ever leave this town alive.

The Kinkaids . . . Fargo abruptly realized this could have been another diversion while 'Bama grabbed the grifters at the hotel. He quickened his pace along the crowded boardwalk, wondering if it was true that you never hear the shot that kills you.

10

It wasn't 'Bama Jones Fargo found waiting back at the hotel room, but a grinning Sheriff Brubaker smoking a smelly cigar. A scattergun was cradled in his arms.

"Fargo!" he greeted the new arrival in a hail-fellow-well-met tone. "Look what the kids have been up to while Daddy's away."

Megan and Julius stood in the center of the room, afraid to meet Fargo's angry eye. One of the two beds had been converted to a poker table, complete with chips and a dealer's bank.

"Seems the little girl here," Lonny narrated, pointing his chin at Megan, "went down into the dining room and cozied up to some high rollers. Invited them up for a private game so her old man could fleece them with his magic hands. Problem is, today is Sunday and we got blue laws in Miller's Bend. No bucking the tiger on Sunday."

"There's gambling right downstairs in the Big Elephant," Megan protested.

Brubaker gave her a cheesy smile. "You must be mistaken, little lady. All laws are vigorously enforced in Miller's Bend."

Fargo felt like shooting the troublesome Kinkaids himself. "You two idiots just had to stoke the fire, didn't you?"

"Skye, you said we could go down to the dining room," Megan argued.

"To *eat.*"

Fargo had another problem in the form of the deputy he'd buffaloed earlier. The man stood just inside the door, and the moment Fargo arrived the deputy had palmed his Volcanic, those black agate eyes hot with barely suppressed rage. His right temple was bruised the color of grapes where Fargo's Colt had beaned him.

"So what's the procedure? I pay a fine directly to you and they go free?"

"No, I'm afraid they'll have to go to jail. After all, they're wanted by several banks. I can't say for sure, however, when the circuit judge will be here to arraign them."

The Kinkaids slanted inploring glances at Fargo, who cursed silently. One part of him wanted to just wash his hands of that larcenous duo; another part couldn't desert them now. Between vicious bounty hunters and this town run by criminals, they were doomed.

"Then again," Brubaker said, "Jake and me haven't searched the room yet. Now, if we happen to come across nine hundred simoleons, maybe we'll leave this room without any prisoners. I'm an amiable man who always prefers the middle way."

The hidebound bag lay on the uncluttered bed. The moment Jake headed toward it, Julius Kinkaid sent Fargo a desperate plea with his eyes.

"Never mind pawing through our gear," Fargo spoke up, pulling a yellow flimsy from his shirt pocket. "The money has been sent back to Plum Creek. Here's a receipt with the amount."

Fargo handed it to Brubaker, who studied it closely. "Yeah, that's Mike Barr's signature. Fargo, have you been grazing loco weed? I would've settled for half that money. Jake, search the bag anyhow."

Fargo's Colt leaped into his fist. The sound was menacing when he thumb-cocked it in the quiet room. "I've had my fill of this high-handed treatment. That bag belongs to me, and I'm not under arrest. I'll plug the first son of a bitch who searches it."

The steel-jawed determination in Fargo's face stayed the other two men from reacting.

"All right, Fargo," Brubaker said. "You win that one. But these two are under legal arrest and they're coming with us."

"Why bother? You know I'm broke, and as a peace

officer you can't collect rewards. They're worth nothing to you."

Brubaker grinned ear to ear. His scattergun was trained on the grifters now. "Wrong. Reed McKinney came to see me today. He'll plank good cash, over the counter, to get the Kinkaids out of my jail. Five hundred dollars apiece."

Brubaker picked up the cash from the bed without counting it and stuffed it in his hip pocket. He nodded toward the hidebound bag. "Now, if you have a thousand dollars in that poke, bring it over to the jail and we'll strike terms."

A hot bustout—the very thing Fargo had feared. He had fought his way out of several towns in sprays of lead, and he hoped to avoid it now. But the Kinkaids made a hard task nearly impossible by getting themselves jugged.

Fargo locked the door, reinforced it with a chair, and untied the rawhide whang holding the bag closed. At first he pulled out nothing of much use, just tools of the confidence and burglary trade: loaded dice, phony stock certificates, implements for picking door and window locks. Then he pulled out a folded-up horse blanket wrapped around something bulky and heavy.

Fargo unwrapped the blanket and, seeing what was secreted within, felt sweat break out on his face. He closed his weary eyes for a long moment and massaged them with his thumbs.

"I'll shoot them both," he informed the room.

Fargo realized it was a miracle he was still alive. Julius was hauling around an explosives magazine with him. Spread out on the bed were a half-dozen "toss-pots," crude bombs filled with black powder and equipped with six-second fuses. They were strictly U.S. Army issue, and Fargo had never seen them in civilian hands.

What truly tightened his scalp, however, were the two one-pound blocks of nitroglycerin. Fargo had worked around railroad crews enough to recognize these as pure nitro oil, extremely volatile. He could tell, from the waxy color, they had been somewhat stabilized by adding an absorbent called kieselguhr so they could be handled and transported. Nonetheless, the stuff was still touchy—a sharp blow could set it off.

"Damn fools," Fargo muttered. Then he paused, thought about the mess he was in, and added, "But needs must when the devil drives."

His calves feeling weak as water, he wrapped the munitions back up and carefully stuffed them into the bag. Then he went down into the late-afternoon heat of Main Street, feeling like first prize in a turkey shoot.

Brubaker's minions worried him, but Reed and 'Bama were back, too, and Fargo would rather face all the devils in hell. He made his way to the jailhouse, a squat log structure halfway down Main. As he had feared, armed thugs buzzed around it like flies on dung.

Fargo moved into a pocket of shade across the street and waited for his chance. It came when one of the thugs arrived from a saloon with a few bottles of red-eye. The rest gathered around him and Fargo was able to slip into an alley and around behind the hoosegow.

Heated voices reached him through a barred window.

"—did *not* call you a whore, I—"

"You'd better not, Daddy dear, or I'll claw your eyeballs out!"

Despite his anger, Fargo was forced to grin. Those two would still be scrapping on the gallows.

"*Psst!* Come down off your hind legs, you two. You won't get out of this jam by tearing at each other's throats."

"Skye." Megan's angelic face appeared in the window, pale with nervous fear. "Thank God you're here!"

"I oughta throw both of you to the wolves. We'd all be playing harps right now if those nitro blocks had gone off."

"We're determined not to get captured," Julius explained.

"Where the hell'd you get that stuff?"

"I stole it from an arsenal in Saint Louis while Megan got the sentries drunk. Given our risky profession, we wanted something dramatic as a last resort. Don't you agree those little toys might help spring us from this cell?"

"They'll help," Fargo agreed, keeping one ear cocked

to the sounds from out front. "But no nitro blocks. We have to avoid killing. The toss-pots should make plenty of catarumpus."

"Why so fastidious about killing *this* bunch?" Julius protested. "They're pond scum."

"True, but even a crooked lawman is still the law. Killing one of them turns *me* into a criminal, and it doesn't help you two either."

"So what's the plan?" Julius demanded. "You know, one of those nitro blocks would take the back wall out of the jail."

"Yeah, and probably kill you two into the deal. I've seen those things blow the wall out of a canyon. No nitro."

"What, then?" Megan pleaded. "Skye, I don't like the way those men are looking at me. They're drinking heavily."

"Yeah, I catch your drift. Look, there's no time for a fancy plan. Either we roll up our sleeves, and quick, or we all stand to lose more than our shirts."

It sounded like the hoisting session around front was breaking up. Fargo spoke quickly. "You two be ready after midnight. My plan will be made up on the fly. Now I've got to git."

With voices approaching the rear of the building, Fargo barely managed to melt into the growing shadows without being spotted. One more item of business remained before he launched this suicide mission, but Fargo realized he would need some sleep before this long night began.

He returned to the hotel, locked and reinforced the door, and flopped onto one of the beds with his weapons to hand.

Under the foxfire glow of a quarter moon, Fargo rode out of Miller's Bend and onto the low bluffs overlooking the Cimarron. His Henry was out of its boot and rested on Fargo's right thigh, muzzle straight up. Several men had seen him leave town, and he couldn't be sure he hadn't been followed.

The air had chilled quickly after sunset, and Fargo's breath made ghostly wraiths. It bothered him, not know-

71

ing where Reed and 'Bama were. Fargo had faced his share of crooked rubes like these townies, but brain-sick killers like McKinney and Jones were a different, more dangerous animal. Reed's words sparked in Fargo's thoughts like burning twigs: *It's the dirt nap for you if you keep helpin' them two.*

Fargo rode to the general area where he had spotted the two Cheyenne earlier today. It was a calculated risk that might get him killed. On the other hand, most Indians appreciated a fair trade. And he had a good offer.

Fargo had calculated the various risks of a bustout from Miller's Bend, and because of the surprise and confusion of explosions, the easiest part should be getting the Kinkaids out of jail. But the surprise element was brief, and the weak point would be the ride out of town and the immediate outskirts. Plenty of men would recover their senses by then and start tossing lead, so Fargo hoped to enlist the Cheyenne as outriders.

The Ovaro shied, whickering in a way Fargo recognized—the stallion had caught a scent of rancid bear grease in the Indians' hair. They were close by but not showing themselves. Fargo knew more Lakota than Cheyenne, but the two groups were cousins and knew each other's language.

"Ready your battle rigs!" he shouted. "I am not here to discuss the causes of the wind. I need warriors!"

Two figures materialized out of the night. The point of a knife jabbed into Fargo's ribs. The Ovaro fought the bit, but Fargo mastered him.

"White men use Indian skulls to prop open the doors of their lodges," a bitter voice spoke in Lakota. "Yet you ride here demanding warriors? What manner of fool are you?"

"You two," Fargo announced boldly, "are from Chief Tangle Hair's camp. The *wasichu* devils who killed your people may soon leave this place before you can kill them and cleanse the sacred arrows of the murder stain."

Fargo respectfully made the cutoff sign for speaking of the dead. He saw the two braves exchange a long glance before the pressure of the knife eased.

"You know much about us, Son of Light," said a

brave wearing the elk-tooth necklace of a subchief. "I am Shoots Left-handed and this is Plenty Coups. We have ears for more."

"It would require you to leave your camp at night," Fargo warned them. "To risk death after dark."

A long silence ensued while each brave looked a question at the other. The night belonged to the Wendigo, to the souls in torment, to *odjib*, the things made of smoke that could not be fought, but would fright a man to death.

"Night?" Plenty Coups finally scoffed. "I can steal a woman from her bed without waking up her husband."

You see a fiery redhead, Fargo silently joked, *fetch her in.*

"Fight where?" Shoots Left-handed demanded. "And who? We are not murderers for hire like the butchers we seek."

"The where," Fargo told them, "is very close to the white man's town below you. You'd be right on the edge."

Fargo knew he was again asking a lot. He had seen few Indians, out West, venture near a town. "Indian fever" often broke out in saloons after drinking sessions, and with the exception of drowning, hanging was the worst way to die for a Cheyenne.

"Fight *who*?" Shoots Left-handed repeated. "We only need to kill our enemies, not yours."

"You know," Fargo said, "that your enemies are following a woman and her father. They are now in jail in the town. I mean to free them this night. If I succeed, your enemy must keep tracking me and remain in your range longer. If they are not freed, your enemies will buy them and leave immediately on a stagecoach."

"This is truth?" Shoots Left-handed asked.

"Straight grain clear through," Fargo assured him.

Both braves were silent, digesting his words.

"If you will help me," Fargo sweetened the deal, "I will promise not to kill either of your enemies unless forced to it."

Plenty Coups looked at his companion. "Son of Light is a *mah-ish-ta-shee-da*, but I trust him. The cold moons are soon upon us. These two devils always leave our homeland during the short white days. We must kill them soon or the Medicine Arrows can never be renewed."

He looked at Fargo. "The two butchers who killed my people—they will be in this fight tonight?"

"Yes. They are here, watching everything."

Again Plenty Coups's fierce face turned to his companion. "Do you hear? It has been too long already since we struck again. Are we girls in our sewing lodge? The monster with the big-talking gun—his flea-bitten scalp will dangle from my sash."

"I trust Son of Light also," Shoots Left-handed said. "But blackening our face for battle in a white man's town—and in darkness? Brother, these things are taboo."

"Then ride to the rear with the cowards! I have no plans to build my death wickiup. I mean to fight!"

Shoots Left-handed gave in. "Plenty Coups is hot-tempered, but he is right—we have been too timid. Better to die than go on watching without action. Hair-face, tell us what we must do."

A huge raft of clouds blew away from the moon, and Fargo studied the jailhouse closely.

Only one man was on guard out front, seated on a nail keg with his North & Savage rifle resting across his thighs. He had companions, however, inside the jailhouse, jollifying themselves with rotgut. Fargo could hear them taunting Megan, their remarks growing coarser as they worked themselves up to rape her.

It was after midnight and Fargo was hidden in a deserted doctor's office across the street from the jail. Earlier, he had retrieved all three horses from the livery and hidden them in an alley just past the jail. Fargo saw men with guns everywhere, so it was hard to know exactly which ones worked for Brubaker. Or who saw him hobble those getaway horses.

Fargo finished throwing dead grass onto the toss-pot he'd planted in a front corner of the slab-lumber building. He stuck his face out a window and glanced each way down the street, making sure it was clear.

"Fargo, how the hell did you get into this?" he muttered as he removed a lucifer from his possibles bag and scratched it to life on the splintery floor.

The six-second fuse spat noisy sparks and Fargo bolted toward a side window he'd already opened, simply diving out as if into water. Only seconds later, abrupt as a thunderclap, the bomb exploded.

Shock froze the guard in place even as blast debris slapped everything around him. Fargo saw oily yellow lantern light leaking from under the door of the jailhouse. His Henry was slung over his left shoulder, his Colt in a firm grip. The moment the door banged open, Fargo crouched low and crossed the shadowy street.

In the initial confusion, the men in the jailhouse—six, by Fargo's count—bolted into the street to gape at the now-burning building. The toss-pot had done impressive damage, Fargo noted. One half of the building's front looked like a giant bite had been taken out of it. Smoldering wood lay in the street, and flames licked toward the sky.

Expecting lead at every moment, Fargo cat-footed down the boardwalk and darted into the jailhouse. He expected a guard and found one, a balding beanpole gaping out the window. Fargo dropped him as he spun around, with a solid right cross to the jaw.

"Skye!" Megan cried out. "I *knew* you'd come!"

"Keep your voice down," he ordered her, "or I'll never *leave*."

Fargo found the key on the desk and let them out. "Our horses are waiting in an alley about fifty yards east of here. Those tin badges left your weapons, but I couldn't tote them with mine. They're in your saddlebags. There'll be a running battle after we hit leather. And one before."

Fargo was peering cautiously out the door while he spoke. With the empty building burning, and the wind kicking up, men had formed a bucket brigade.

"All right," he told his unwelcome charges, "here's the way of it. This right now is the hard part—getting horsed and out of town. It's not just the peckerwoods outside. I think the bounty hunters will pitch into the game, too."

Fargo waved Julius up to the door first. "I saw you

sneak-foot into the Plum Creek bank, and you were slick. You'll go first. When you get to the alley, get the hobbles off our horses. Megan's next, with me right behind her."

Julius swallowed audibly. "Yes, I know I can do this."

"You'll do to take along," Fargo assured him. "I never saw a man stay so frosty under fire as you did when McKinney and Jones jumped you. Easy to see how you won that duel in New Orleans. Just remember, if you're spotted run like a scalded dog, and keep running. A gun is useless to you at this point—there's too many trained against us."

Julius nodded, cast a brief glance at Megan, and glided out into the fire-lit, raucous night.

"My lands, look at all those armed men gathering," Megan fretted. "How will we possibly sneak past them?"

"Just remember what I told your dad. We won't risk running unless they see us, and then we run like hell."

"Skye! I'm not sure I can—"

"Well, I'm sure you can. You stood right alongside your father in that attack. Now get ready before they send somebody back over here. I'll be right behind you . . . *go!*"

The moment Megan stepped out, however, somebody across the street shouted, "Jailbreak!"

"Keep going!" Fargo urged Megan when she halted, unsure what to do. He slipped an arm around her and propelled her forward. "Hold on to me and try to keep up!"

Megan screamed when the initial volley opened up. So many rifles and handguns detonated at once that the barrage sounded like an ice floe breaking apart. Rounds pinged in on all sides, kicking up plumes all around their feet.

"That's Skye Fargo with her!" roared the deep voice of Jake, the deputy Fargo had knocked out earlier. "Kill that egg-suckin' varmint!"

Fargo had experienced plenty of withering fire, and this rated right up there among terrifying experiences. Bullets chewed wood all around them, shattered windows, stirred the street to dust clouds. He was caught between the sap and the bark—if he let go of Megan, at this speed, she'd tumble. Yet, by hanging on to her he couldn't return effective fire.

He chose to hang on, bullets be damned. It seemed a miracle when they reached the mouth of the alley. Julius held the horses ready.

The enraged townies had given pursuit, and Fargo heard them pounding closer.

"Come here and mount up," he snapped at Megan. "They're almost on us."

But Megan, on the feather edge of panic after that shooting gallery, wasn't listening.

"*Mount*," Fargo told her again, desperation spiking his voice. Cursing, he slapped her face and tossed her into the saddle. Her horse shied toward the street. Muscles straining like guy ropes, Fargo restrained the mare from bolting.

"Get going!" Fargo shouted to Julius. "I'll try to slow them down and catch up with you. Keep an eye on her—she's gone battle simple."

Fargo slapped the mare's glossy rump and shrugged the Henry off his shoulder, levering a round up. As fast as he could, he squeezed off rounds, not trying to pop over any targets, just to scare the mob. It sent them to cover or back into town for their mounts.

The moment the hammer clicked on an empty chamber, Fargo vaulted into the saddle, booted his rifle, and heeled the Ovaro's ribs, bearing due east behind his companions. Riders already thundered behind him, and more gunshots punctuated the night.

The two Cheyenne, however, had kept their word. They waited right where Fargo told them to, in a copse near the road about five hundred yards outside of town. He heard their yipping cries as they attacked, heard them mocking their enemies with shouts. The panicked cry, "Injins!" went up, considerably thinning out the ranks of the pursuers. Fargo enjoyed a brief grin: this close to the Indian Territory, all white settlers feared a bloody uprising.

The Ovaro laid back his ears and stretched out at a powerful gait, outdistancing the distracted pursuers with ease. However, Fargo felt his heart leap into his throat when he peered intently into the darkness ahead: Julius and Megan were fleeing at a gallop, Reed McKinney and 'Bama Jones almost close enough to grab their horses' tails.

Fargo cursed, skinning his Colt. At this distance and gait, he'd never score hits with a handgun. Maybe the noise would help.

Fargo never had to pull the trigger. Obviously Julius had gotten into the hidebound bag, and now he played his ace. Fargo saw a spray of sparks suddenly arc from his horse as he lobbed a toss-pot over his shoulder.

It hit, bounced once, and blew up in the road, a wall of dirt slamming up into Reed and 'Bama. Both horses went down in nickering fright, their riders barely keeping their legs from being pinned.

Fargo flashed past, not even trying to get a bead, only trying to catch up with the Kinkaids. Against all odds, this bustout just might succeed. Fargo had looked closely, however, at McKinney and Jones, and neither man appeared seriously hurt. The worst was yet to come.

11

While the moon clawed higher toward its zenith, the three riders continued fleeing toward the east. Fargo gauged the time by judging the height of the dawn star in the east. Finally, exhausted and powder-blackened, he reined in and swung down, kneeling to feel the ground with his fingertips.

"No pursuers," he announced. "But this isn't a good place to camp. We'll keep moving."

Soon, ghostly white tines of lightning shot down from the sky and howling winds buffeted them, but they pushed on. Finally they reached a well-protected hollow beside a stream and made camp.

All three stripped tack from their wet and tired mounts.

"It ain't over," Fargo warned. "Not by a long shot. You rattled those bounty hunters with that toss-pot, but they won't give up until a bullet persuades them."

"What's the plan now?" Megan asked.

"Kansas City," Fargo replied. "It's a few days' ride northeast of here. There's railroad and stage connections to back east, steamboats headed south. It's going to be a rough ride, though. McKinney and Jones will be dogging our heels. There's also roving bands of Jayhawkers, and they'll have a special interest in you, Megan."

"One thing I don't understand," Julius said. "Right at the edge of Miller's Bend we had a horde of berserkers about to engulf us, then they backed off. What happened?"

"I palavered with those two Cheyenne. They did a little flanking assault. Caught our brave 'citizens' militia' by surprise and scared the vinegar out of 'em. Prob'ly figured they had an Indian uprising on their hands. Now we owe those two braves."

It was about two hours until sunrise. Fargo had gathered enough sticks for a fire. He pulled a handful of crumbled bark from a pannier to use as kindling.

"Elijah's rations will tide us well on the trail," Fargo said. "Sourdough biscuits and bacon, coming up."

"Sounds like a feast," Megan said. "I'm going down to the stream to wash up."

"Fargo," Julius said after she left, "my eternal thanks for saving her back there. We've been in some tight spots before, but I never saw her freeze up like that."

"Hell," Fargo replied, "she was caught in a hailstorm of lead. I think it was the noise that unstrung her nerves. You're a damn fool to expose her to the risks of a criminal existence. That girl should be married to some Philadelphia lawyer, not ducking bullets in jerkwater towns."

Julius sighed. "Truer words and all that. I swear, from now on I live on the road called Straight. That girl has shilled for me for the last time. And I'm going back to teaching school."

"Sounds good," Fargo agreed. "But that's *if* you survive McKinney and Jones. Speaking of skunk-bit coyotes—here, watch this bacon. I'm taking a squint around."

Fargo's Henry leaned against a cottonwood. He grabbed it and walked a circle around the hollow, looking and listening in the darkness. It was so quiet he could hear Megan splashing in the stream. He walked over that way, spotting her in the dim but gathering light.

"Damn," Fargo muttered, his arousal instant.

Megan stood in thigh-deep water, sudsing her breasts and flat, creamy stomach. Even in the stingy light he could make out her dark nipples.

"Come closer," she called out, spotting him. Her husky tone made it clear she was as ready as Fargo.

He wavered, glancing over his shoulder. "I don't know. Your father—"

Fargo's words stuck in his throat like unchewed bread when he turned his head back around. Megan had hurried to the grassy, sloping bank and now lay on her back, legs scissored open wide.

"Please?" she teased him. "Just a quick one? You were so brave tonight, and I want to thank you—properly."

"Hell," Fargo surrendered. "I don't want to be impolite."

He crossed to her in several rapid strides, grounded the Henry, and unbuckled his gun belt. While he worked at the belt, Megan's lust-trembling fingers worked open his fly and freed his straining shaft.

"I've never felt one this big," she whispered, stroking him in a tight fist. "It's exciting. You're a stallion, Skye Fargo."

She stroked faster, and Fargo felt tickling fire in his groin.

"Give it to me, Skye!" she begged, her breath hot and airy in his ear. "Do me hard! I don't want to think, just feel pleasure."

Fargo found her nest wet and ready. He parted the elastic walls of her sex as he thrust into her, both of them gasping at the powerful thrill.

"This is all I've been thinking about since our first time," she whispered. "Do me, Skye, *do* me!"

At times like this Fargo welcomed bossy women. He thrust hard and fast, so vigorously that Megan slid across the grass a little with each thrust. She keened with pleasure, wrapping her legs around him and locking her ankles behind his back. Luscious tits mashed into Fargo, soft but firm, and the talented wriggling of her hips made sure all of his aroused member was pleasured.

"Oh, Skye, I'm going to *explode*!" she gasped, her thrashing climax triggering Fargo's. They moaned together in deep release.

"Where are you two?" Julius's peevish voice called out.

Fargo cursed in a whisper as he rose to his knees, tied the flap of his fly closed, and buckled on his gun belt. "You get dressed while I head back from a different angle. He *is* your father, after all."

"Skye?" she called behind him as he started to leave.

"You think McKinney and Jones are going to kill us, don't you?"

Fargo sent her a cross-shoulder glance. "They're going to try, sure."

"Then I'm especially glad for what we did just now. If I have to die young, I'd rather taste some pleasure before I go."

Her strong spirit showed even in her voice. Fargo grinned. "That's a philosophy I believe and practice."

"Oh, yes, you've had plenty of practice. It shows."

"That a complaint?"

She laughed, drying her hair with a scrap of towel. "No, sir, it is not."

"Fargo!" Julius brayed. "Megan, where are you?"

"Drying my hair!" she replied as Fargo slipped away.

12

As he rolled into his blanket, during the brief camp at the hollow, Fargo didn't believe even the resourceful McKinney and Jones could have caught up to them yet. He suspended any guard duty for this two-hour sleep, which meant the Kinkaids slept while he went into a frontier half-sleep—his body went heavy but his senses stayed aware.

Fargo heard coyotes again, and wondered if it was the brain-sick Reed mocking them. He dozed with his gun belt on and woke up so tired he wished he'd simply stayed awake.

The new day, however, dawned promising; with a clear horizon on all sides. They struck their simple camp and Fargo helped Megan into the saddle.

"We'll rest the horses plenty," he told the other two. "They had a hard run back there, and this rest was too short. Just hope that anybody chasing us is on a spent horse. Lead tends to fly around us."

Fargo forked leather and heeled the Ovaro forward.

"We should have bypassed Miller's Bend altogether," Julius said. "I'm a born fool, but you should have known better, Fargo."

"You're right," Fargo agreed, "but it's too dead to skin. We're *all* outlaws on the prod. All we can do is hightail it."

Toward the end of the day they stopped at a pond beside a cottonwood with a lightning-split trunk. Late-afternoon sunlight formed a shimmering haze over low, distant hills to the north. From where Fargo stood they looked like a pod of whales.

Within an hour they rode in sight of a rough-and-tumble-looking crossroads settlement. Telegraph wires, however, sent Fargo looping wide around it.

"Might be honest law there," Megan suggested. "After all, you said McKinney and Jones murder to get new horses. Maybe somebody here will arrest them."

"Uh-huh," her father said scornfully. "And oysters can walk upstairs, can't they? Woman, Skye is now a wanted man. *He* can't go to the law."

"Your old man's talking sense," Fargo said. "There's honest law out west, but the Kansas Territory ain't the place to expect it."

With the last light of day bleeding from the sky, the Trailsman selected a campsite on the south bank of the Arkansas where it bowed just west of the settlement of Jeffordsville.

"Somebody's riding this way," Megan said, her voice tight with nervous tension.

Julius, too, discerned the approaching silhouette and drew his revolver.

"Hold your powder," Fargo said. "It's the Cheyenne named Shoots Left-handed. He's been following us for a long time."

"I thought he had long hair," Megan said when the brave had ridden closer in the fading light. "Both of them."

"Cheyenne cut short their hair to mourn their dead," Fargo explained. "It's a good bet that McKinney or Jones killed his friend Plenty Coups."

Shoots Left-handed approached the camp with his free hand held up to show he carried no weapon. He studied all of them from calm and fathomless eyes.

"Before you *wasichus* came upon us like locusts," he greeted Fargo in a bitter tone, "there were always two fires burning in my lodge. One for food and one for friendship. But the friendship fire is no more!"

Fargo shook his head. "I have no ears for these words. Do *I* demand that you grow gardens and wear shoes? I live much like the red man myself."

The Cheyenne nodded reluctantly. "Straight words. This thing we have spoken of—do you understand now?

How it is more important than ever that *I* kill the butchers, not you?"

"I hope it is you," Fargo admitted. "They're both sick in the mind, the worst kind of murderers."

"They are approaching this place," the brave warned him. "I raced ahead to tell you. They are like iron men in the saddle. They rarely stop. They have killed my battle cousin, but I no longer fear them. I have sung the strong-heart songs and prayed these men into the ground. Now, for me, it is glory or a funeral scaffold."

Or both, Fargo thought, watching the determined brave ride off.

"What was that all about?" Julius asked.

Fargo translated, adding, "It's nothing I didn't know anyway, except the part about killing Plenty Coups. McKinney and Jones will stay on us like ugly on a buzzard."

"Do you think Shoots Left-handed can kill those two?" Megan asked.

"He's a Cheyenne and a blooded warrior, a subchief. He's got as much chance as anybody. But I'm not counting on it. All three of us have to be ready for the attack. We'll go back to guard shifts tonight. But neither one of you leaves the camp circle."

Fargo stripped the Ovaro's neck leather while he spoke. "They're desperate now, and they know that the best way to stop us, in this country, is to put us afoot. We'll let the horses graze farther out for now, then tether them near our bedrolls when we turn in. Check the loads in your weapons and stay right here."

"Skye?" Megan said. "What if nature calls during the night?"

"Personally," Fargo replied, "I rate staying alive higher than I rate modesty. Pee close by or hold it until daylight."

Fargo ruled out a fire, so they ate cold biscuits and shared a can of peaches Fargo opened with his Arkansas toothpick. Despite the warning from Shoots Left-handed, the night passed peacefully. When it was his turn to sleep, Fargo tied the nearby Ovaro to his wrist, but there was no warning tug to wake him.

"Maybe they gave us up as a bad job," Julius suggested next morning over hot coffee. "Or that Cheyenne buck killed them."

"They could be dead," Fargo agreed. "But they didn't give up. They don't go after any bounty unless it's big."

Fargo stood a little apart from the other two, his weather-tanned face turned to the horizon, lake blue eyes missing nothing. He watched for movement, not shapes, for at great distances it was motion that caught the eye. Fargo also watched for dust puffs, reflections, or startled birds.

"Unless they're lying in grass to ambush us," Fargo finally said, "it's clear out there, for now. Let's make tracks."

A pale sun rose higher, gathering heat as it burned off the dew. They trekked across a vast, flat plain, the grass lush in spots, spotty as an old hide in others.

"Sheep grazed here," Fargo explained. "Took the grass out roots and all. Cattle and horses only eat the top. Gonna be bad trouble over that someday soon."

By late afternoon Fargo's head constantly swiveled to glance behind them.

"Trouble?" Julius asked.

"Could be. We've got riders trailing us."

Megan groaned. "McKinney and Jones."

"That's not a hard-cash fact it's them," Fargo reminded her. "Could be anybody."

All three riders were still holding a trot. Fargo said, "I'll go take a look. Soon as I leave, you two open it out to a lope. I'll catch up."

Just as Fargo fell silent, the crack of a distant rifle split the silence.

"Not again!" Megan protested.

"Wasn't aimed at us," Fargo said. "Get going now."

He reined around and chucked the Ovaro up to a canter, pulling his Henry from its boot and holding it balanced on the pommel. Fargo knew it was virtually impossible, without taking hours to do it, to sneak up on plainsmen like McKinney and Jones. So he simply bore directly toward the specks following him, intending to get a good look.

Soon he could make out two men riding at a brisk trot. The giant on the claybank had to be 'Bama Jones, and the smaller man on the sorrel was Reed McKinney. Reed had a fresh-killed rabbit tied to his saddle horn, which probably explained the rifle shot.

"Didn't take you bloodthirsty sons of bitches long to get back on the scent," Fargo muttered.

He took no pains to turn and flee. His enemies were excellent trackers and knew their quarry was close. He watched Reed pull field glasses out and study him. Only when both bounty hunters spurred their mounts forward did Fargo head back.

"Let's get thrashing, boys," he muttered before whistling to the Ovaro.

He opened the stallion out to a gallop and overtook the Kinkaids.

"Bounty hunters closing in!" he shouted above the pounding of hooves. "I deliberately drew them out; this is the best place to face them. Head for that low ridge with the boulders on it."

Fargo whistled and slapped the Ovaro's rump with his hat, urging the pinto to winged speed. Their pursuers were still well back, but a few rounds were ranging in, ripping divots out of the grass and sod.

Then, in a heart-stopping instant, Fargo watched their odds for survival literally drop when, with a sickening crack of breaking bone, Megan's chestnut mare went tumbling to the ground. Fargo saw the splintered bone in the mare's foreleg, which had plunged into a hidden gopher hole.

Julius cried out when he saw his daughter flung hard to the ground, so hard that she bounced and rolled like a child's toy. He reined in with Fargo.

"Get to the ridge!" Fargo shouted to him as he leaped down and put a bullet in the screaming horse to end her suffering. "I'll bring Megan. Hurry, Kinkaid, those rounds are finding targets now!"

Behind them, the two killers saw this golden opportunity and whooped in triumph. They pounded ever closer, chucking a wall of lead before them.

"Dust!" Fargo ordered Julius again. The Trailsman

leaned over Megan, expecting the worst. A big knot was already swelling up where her forehead had hit the ground. However, her eyes fluttered open briefly.

Julius crowded close. "Fargo! Is she—"

Fargo grabbed the man's lapels and shook him until his teeth clacked. "Damn you, get to those rocks! I need you to take my Henry and lay down covering fire so I can get Megan to safety. If we get trapped here, they'll cut us to rag tatters."

As if to make Fargo's point, a bullet whanged off the ground and spun Kinkaid's hat off his head. That snapped him back to reality.

"I'll make it lively for them," he promised. "Good luck, Fargo."

Now, Fargo realized, came the truly hard part. Under withering fire he had to pick up Megan, lift her into the saddle, and then *keep* her there while still escaping from determined pursuers who were dead aims. To protect Megan, Fargo kept her in front of him when he swung up. A bullet kissed the left stirrup, barely missing his foot. Others whistled and hissed all around them.

"Let's see you shit fire, old warhorse!" Fargo shouted above the racket, giving the Ovaro a sharp squeeze with his knees. "Hell's a-poppin'!"

13

In times of trouble Fargo had learned to stop the flow of thoughts and attend only to the language of his senses. As he urged the Ovaro toward the low, rocky ridge, he let his ears, and ground vibrations, tell him exactly how close the pursuers were.

His ears also told him when Reed McKinney switched from the lever-action rifle with the buckskin patch to his six-guns—weapons with which he was a supreme master. If McKinney had skinned his short guns, it meant he was confident of a kill, and Fargo's back was a broad target.

"Hii-ya!" Fargo urged the game but overburdened Ovaro. "Hii-*ya!*"

The ridge loomed dead ahead; however, with rounds blurring the air, it still seemed agonizingly distant to Fargo. Julius had reached cover up there but was unfamiliar with the Henry. His shots were not well placed, but at least he was making a lot of noise.

"Skye!" Megan cried, regaining consciousness. "What's going on?"

"Cider party, hon. Can you grab the saddle horn?"

"I—I think so. Why?"

"When I give the word, you just hang on tight."

Fargo knew it was down to the black flag now. Fading daylight helped some, but in mere moments McKinney would be in effective handgun range. Fargo had saved his Colt for the final push onto the ridge. If Megan could hang on long enough, he could torque around in the saddle and fire back.

"You're dog meat, Fargo!" came a triumphant shout from behind him. "Now you're goin' to glory, Trailsman!"

A .36 Navy cracked, a round grazed Fargo's saddle fender, and he shouted, "Now, Megan! Hold on for dear life!"

With the reins bunched in his left hand, Fargo whipped halfway around in the saddle, shucking out his Colt as he did so. Reed McKinney, hunched low in the saddle, was drawing a bead, 'Bama pounding close behind him. Fargo unloaded six shots just as fast as he could cock and fire the single-action weapon.

Firing from a galloping horse, Fargo scored no hits. However, his rounds flew close enough to rattle the bounty hunters and buy a few precious seconds. Fargo raced onto the ridge and joined Julius behind a cluster of boulders.

"Your rifle's empty," the grifter reported from a powder-blackened face as Fargo helped Megan to cover. "And they're headed right up here!"

"Use your short gun," Fargo snapped. "*Don't* let 'Bama get close enough to unlimber that multishot meat grinder of his."

Julius drew the revolver from his waistband and opened fire while Fargo, willing his fingers steady, reloaded the Henry's cumbersome tube magazine.

"Christ, Fargo, take your sweet old time!" Kinkaid said. "I'm down to my derringer now!"

Fargo didn't need the dire report—bullets were splatting from rock to rock as they ricocheted, striking sparks. But once Fargo got the Henry chattering again, both bounty hunters wisely retreated.

"Reload both handguns," Fargo ordered Julius, tossing his Colt over to him. "And grab Megan's gun. These two roaches are hard to predict, but they ain't done with us yet."

The ridge offered some safety, but without water and graze it was a poor place to camp. Nonetheless, Fargo knew they were stuck there. Night was settling in, but worse, they were down to two horses and would never outpace these stone-hearted killers across open plains.

"Can you see them?" Julius asked, watching Fargo study the plains to their west.

Fargo nodded. "They're camping in plain sight of us. Rubbing it in."

"If it's not safe up here," Megan said, "I'm well enough to ride."

Fargo glanced at her. She was still woozy, and a nasty bruise had swollen her forehead.

"Best to stick for now," he told her. "Why push if a thing won't move? We're down to two horses, and they're played out."

"But there's no water here," Julius pointed out. "The horses need water more than rest, don't they?"

"They've been watered regularly since we rode out from up north. We've still got our canteens. We'll give each horse a few swallows from our hats. Water isn't scarce in this region—we'll make it up."

Fargo stared at the sawing orange flames of the bounty hunters' camp, tasting bitter bile. He had come to manhood when the West was still pristine and its few inhabitants at one with the wild. The buffalo herds were so vast it sometimes took a full day for one to pass by. Indians found whites amusing, not dangerous. Now, however, the shining times were over. Railroads, mines, banks, dams, all ensured that men like McKinney and Jones would grow fat off killing, while the wild landscape was destroyed for profit.

Julius's voice sliced into his thoughts. "They've got us, haven't they? Trapped up here where they want us? They know we have to run out of water and ammo."

"So do they."

"Yes, but—"

"I never let my enemy determine my fate," Fargo said, letting some light into this dark situation. "Sure, they won the opening round. But all that matters is who's left standing when the final smoke clears. We won't be staying up here."

"Well, I hope you're right, Fargo. But it's going to be a long night, and *this* gambler needs a couple aces in reserve."

Julius rooted in the hide bag and produced two of the toss-pots, setting them behind a boulder.

Fargo nodded approval. "Good idea. It's that damn

nitro you two are fools to carry. A dirty look will set it off."

"No, you're thinking of pure nitro oil that hasn't been stabilized like these. These blocks require a detonator cap."

"They're partially stabilized," Fargo corrected. "So they can be shipped and handled. Not *man*handled."

"They might come in handy before we're out of this mess," Julius coaxed.

Fargo gazed at the distant fire. "Actually, they might at that," he agreed softly.

Complete darkness settled over them in the next half hour. There was no wood for a fire, but the rations they'd purchased at Donaldson's trading post furnished a tolerable meal of salt pork and hardtack. Fargo showed the other two how to find clean rainwater in the hollows of rocks, saving more canteen water for the Ovaro and the palomino.

"My stomach's on fire," Julius complained. "Nervous digestion. I wish I had some of that new canned milk of Gail Borden's."

"I've tasted it," Fargo said. "It's only good in coffee."

Megan lay on her blanket and groundsheet, quieter than usual. With her next question, Fargo realized why.

"Skye, they haven't attacked again, and it's been several hours. They're waiting until well after dark, aren't they?"

"With those two," Fargo told her, "you just can't know. A lot depends on how much ammunition they're packing along. They've sent plenty of lead our way in the past few days. Could be they're waiting until dawn when we set out. After all, it's easier to pick off targets in the open than to flush them from cover."

"Thanks," she said despondently. "I was hoping for just such a lift."

Fargo laughed. "You two are already picking flowers for our graves. You got the wrong attitude for coming west. Me, I *always* expect to see the next sunrise. The quickest way to waste your life is to always be worrying about when it's going to end."

"Hard not to at times like this."

"Pee doodles," Fargo scoffed. "Once you mate with

despair, you're a gone-up case. Those two out there are only men, not tin gods, and they bleed like all the rest."

"Homey frontier philosophy," Julius told his daughter, his tone dripping irony.

"No," Fargo corrected him, "that's called truth with the bark still on it."

Deciding Megan needed rest, Fargo switched off on guard duty with Julius throughout the night. Time ticked off uneventfully until well past midnight. Then, with no warning, Fargo heard Reed's voice break the silence.

"Hallo, Fargo! You humpin' that little cottontail or sleeping? Me, I'm gonna poke her until she sees God."

Fargo, his back to a boulder, almost leaped out of his buckskins. McKinney was only about fifty yards out, Fargo judged, but even the Ovaro had not detected him. He had proven his great skill at stealth.

His disembodied voice spoke again out of the darkness: "Fargo! Let's me and you make medicine, boy."

"You're here, say your piece." Fargo lowered his voice and told the others, "Megan, cock your gun and put your back to a boulder. Julius, use those sharp eyes to watch for 'Bama. Reed could be a diversion."

"Just this, quim stealer. Besides the sweet lovin', the hell you care about them Kinkaids? By now you already trimmed the high-hatting slut, and I hear tell how the great Trailsman gets his bell rope pulled more than ten men."

"Plenty of practice, right?" Megan whispered to Fargo.

"Said pot to the kettle," Julius nailed her.

"You morally depraved—!"

"Do you two mind?" Fargo growled. "Shut up and watch for Jones."

Reed's voice said, "How's 'bout it, Fargo? Give 'em to us and we'll give you a thousand dollars. That'll stake you to plenty of poker games."

Fargo stood beside a waist-high boulder, his head in constant motion as he watched the darkness. Clouds obscured moon and stars, a perfect time for 'Bama to go prowling with that demonic weapon of his.

"Give it to me when?" Fargo demanded, feeling both

Kinkaids stare poison daggers at him. "Right when I hand them over?"

"Katy Christ, Fargo, we don't carry that kind of money. You'll get it when we collect our reward."

"Funny. That's not what you told Lonny Brubaker back in Miller's Bend. It was cash over the counter with him."

Reed laughed. "Ahh, you know how it is. That bunch in Miller's Bend are two-bit suckers—they'll swallow anything. Wha'd'ya say, Fargo, let's spit on it."

It was Fargo's turn to laugh, one deeper and more genuine than Reed's. "McKinney, you weasels are all alike. If money was my game, I'd cash them in myself."

"Then how 'bout this, big man. Give 'em to us and we won't kill you."

"McKinney?"

"Yeah?"

"Where's 'Bama?"

Reed sniggered. "That boy was right here a minute ago. Could be he went to take a crap. See, ol' 'Bama eats like a winter-starved bear, and craps all day when he ain't killin'."

"If he's headed our way," Fargo told Reed, "he'll get a mighty warm reception. Goes for both of you."

Fargo held his Colt at the ready and quickly moved to a new position downridge, dropping to all fours to watch just above the ground, looking for leg shapes in motion.

"I'll repeat my last offer, Fargo, the best you're going to get. Give us the Kinkaids right now and we won't kill you. You can just ride off, lady-killer, and get you some fine-haired quiff somewhere else."

Fargo stood up, rotating as he walked, eyes to all sides, ears primed. "I got a counteroffer, headhunter. The Kinkaids stay with me and I kill both of you."

"Eat shit and go naked, Fargo, you *had* your chance! It's comin' down to me and you now!"

'Bama had been with Reed all along. As they headed back to their camp, Reed said, "The best chink in their armor is the girl. We saw that today when her horse went down. They lose speed now."

Reed heard a stick snap, and both Colts filled his fists in a heart skip.

"Anyhow," he went on, eyes prowling the darkness, "we were fools to count on those hiders for anything. There's some old boys in the Kansas Territory who know 'b' from a bull's foot. And I know where to find 'em."

14

Dawn broke over the plains in its full glory, a salmon pink glow on the horizon that soon turned to burnished gold. Pockets of mist floated like gossamer clouds.

"My stars, what a miserable night," Megan complained.

She sat wrapped in her blanket, teeth chattering. The terrible shrieking of the north wind had rubbed their nerves raw and left them shivering.

"It'll heat up quick," Fargo assured her. "The bitter cold is still six weeks or so off."

Julius heard them talking and rolled out of his blanket, rumpled and yawning. "I kept waiting all night for that damn shotgun to open up. Those lowdown sons of bitches still camped nearby?"

Fargo shook his head. "But they'll be out there waiting for us. We *do* have company nearby, though."

Fargo pointed north, where a lone Cheyenne brave sat his pony. He faced east and began a haunting, sing-song chant.

"What is he doing?" Megan asked.

"Singing the 'Song to the New Sun Rising.' He's hoping to get strength from the sun."

"I don't get it," Julius said. "Why doesn't he just attack them, if his bloodlust is so powerful? He had a chance last night when they were camped on open ground. Is he trying to work up his courage?"

"He's afraid, all right, but not of dying. He's afraid he'll fail and condemn his people to utter destruction. The bounty hunters have already killed his companion.

With those two, he knows he'll probably get only one chance. So it has to be a good one."

"Why would the tribe be destroyed if McKinney and Jones aren't killed?" Megan asked.

"Way they see it, killing those two cleanses their sacred Medicine Arrows of blood, a symbolic purging of the people's guilt and sins."

"Foolish nonsense," Julius scoffed.

"Funny," Fargo said. "That's what most Indians think about a virgin having a baby."

The Cheyenne finished his prayer song and rode toward the new sun.

Fargo had stocked up on oats in Miller's Bend, and both horses were fed a hatful. Fargo and the Kinkaids then ate some hardtack and dried fruit for breakfast.

"Those two jackals are out there waiting for us," Fargo repeated. "They know we're down to two horses, and they mean to jump us in the open and run us to ground. So I scratched up a little plan."

He looked at Julius. "You have a slight build. How much you weigh?"

"About a hundred and forty pounds."

"All right, and Megan is a mere slip of a girl."

"I guess you'd know, Fargo," Kinkaid remarked dryly.

Megan's nostrils flared. "Get over your peeve, poncy man. What I do is my business."

Fargo gave a long, fluttering sigh. "Going insane, the whole damn world. Like I was saying, both of you are light. That palomino is young and strong. You two will ride double, and it'll be no more weight than a big man. That leaves me free to ride roving skirmisher between you and the bounty hunters."

"Ride with *him*?" Megan protested. "I'd rather walk."

"Good," her father said. "I'll have my own horse."

"This ain't a debate," Fargo snapped. "You'll ride double."

They rigged their horses, checked their weapons, and rode down off the rocky ridge onto the flat, green, endless plains of the eastern Kansas Territory.

Fargo halted his companions to make a careful study of the land. He sent his gaze across the entire vista, studying and reading the shadows. Then he turned sideways and studied it with peripheral vision. This sometimes revealed shapes and movements that direct vision could not.

"See them?" Julius asked.

Fargo shook his head. "No, but that's only because they're so good at concealment. They're out there, all right. Watching, waiting, just like a couple of buzzards. Let's make tracks."

Fargo opted for holding the Ovaro to a fast trot, a good pace that most horses could handle for hours. At the first creek they reached, they filled their canteens and let the horses tank up.

"Keep your eyes peeled now," Fargo warned them. "The ground has folds in it that give cover. I think we're about to have uninvited company."

Once again Fargo's survival instincts proved sound. Less than thirty minutes after they left the creek, the trap was sprung. To left and right of the three riders, a man and horse suddenly seemed to rise out of the very ground, pounding toward them at a gallop.

"Classic pincers trap," Fargo told his white-faced companions. "Julius, ki-yi that palomino straight ahead at a lope. Stay frosty and remember you both have guns if anything happens to me. Don't let them take you."

Fargo stayed behind as a screen between the Kinkaids and the bounty hunters. Both killers hurtled toward him, horses' hooves throwing up chunks of prairie sod. Fargo speared the Henry from its boot and set to work with precision, rotating first left, then right, refusing to give quarter even when Reed sent a wild flurry of bullets from a buckskin-patched rifle.

Reed whooped a signal, and he and 'Bama tore off ahead, each charging a flank of the Kinkaids.

However, Fargo had anticipated the move. One of the Ovaro's great skills was cutting and dodging—like a born cow pony, the stallion could stop on a quarter and give fifteen cents in change. Fargo relied on that great skill now to save human lives.

As the pincers closed, the Ovaro nimbly darted between flanks as Fargo covered both sides with the Henry, interrupting and then turning back the attackers.

It was a hard contest between horses, and the Ovaro was winning.

Until disaster struck. Fargo's stallion was making another fast cut, changing directions to charge at 'Bama. But the pinto's right foreleg went down on a patch of wet grass, and Fargo too crashed hard and fast to the ground, the slam like a mule kick.

Fargo's mind played cat and mouse with awareness. He felt the ground shuddering under him as 'Bama's horse thundered closer, heard the sick killer's victory roar.

Megan's terrified voice: "Skye! Skye, wake *up*!"

Reed: "You *got* him, bo! Grind the bastard to stew meat!"

The horse raced closer, hooves beating a tattoo of impending death. Memory flexed a muscle, time suddenly shifted back to the present, and it was over quicker than a bad dream as Fargo came to his feet, the life instinct strong and aggressive.

He was only seconds away from being trampled by 'Bama's big claybank. Fargo had no time to think, only to act. He had once watched a Sioux, trapped afoot in open country, use a daring move to bring down an attacker's horse. Fargo copied it now from memory, crouching low, an eyeblink before being crushed, and tackling both of the horse's forelegs hard.

The claybank tumbled and skidded across the grass, 'Bama bounced like a child's ball, and Fargo came rolling onto his heels with only a few scrapes. However, there was no time to dispatch 'Bama—Reed had charged the Kinkaids with both six-shooters blazing. They were gamely firing back, but Reed's lethal accuracy could not be contested.

The Ovaro stood a few yards away, still snorting from his fall. Fargo speared his Henry off the ground, vaulted into the saddle, and made a beeline toward the bounty hunter, standing up in the stirrups to bust caps. Caught in a crossfire, Reed peeled off to a safe distance. 'Bama was still on the ground, and his partner knew this hand had gone to the enemy.

"Savor it, Fargo, you crusading son of a bitch!" Reed

bellowed. "The worm *will* turn, you hear me? I'll pickle your head in brine!"

"Fargo," Julius Kinkaid said, "I expected to see strange and marvelous sights when I journeyed west, and I most certainly have. I've seen savages in war paint, lynchings, bands of mounted criminals controlling entire towns. But *never* will anyone believe me when I tell them I saw a man tackle a galloping horse. Perhaps you could do it again, think? Why, I'll have tickets printed—"

"Tell you what," Fargo cut him off. "You tackle the next one, then it's my turn again."

"Just a thought."

Megan, reluctantly riding groom's seat behind her father, spoke up in a goading tone. "We didn't *journey* west, Father. We fled from an angry mob in Ohio, remember? After your 'miracle cure for all ailments known to man or cattle' gave an entire village the trots?"

"That was an innocent mistake," Kinkaid protested. "I gave them purgative instead of curative. I should have marked the barrels. At any rate, as I was saying, Fargo . . ."

The Trailsman filtered most of this prattle out, senses trained in all directions. It had been more than two hours since the attempt by McKinney and Jones, and Fargo hadn't seen a sign of trouble.

That bothered him. He welcomed the peace but feared what such a hiatus foreshadowed. True, they had rebuffed the bounty hunters every time, but both were still alive and sassy. The loss of their horses, a bomb, vengeful Cheyenne—so far nothing had stopped their quest for a good bounty. They were those rare creatures, bullies who were not cowards, and Reed, at least, had a good think-piece on him. They were dangerous, and Fargo respected danger even if he didn't respect them.

His eyes stayed in slow, scanning motion. Fargo didn't try to spot focus, but simply let the entire landscape flow up to his eyes. Long ago he had learned that scouting was much more than simply looking. Each different terrain required its own techniques, and with the exception of deserts, open plains were the most demanding. The complete lack of reference points overwhelmed sight.

"Maybe the big one got hurt," Megan said hopefully. "He fell hard when you tackled his horse. That could explain why we haven't seen them again."

"It's possible," Fargo agreed. "But not wise to count on it."

He led them northeast in the brittle sunlight, nerves steeled for whatever was coming.

15

A westering sun threw long, flat shadows to the east. For long hours the three riders on two horses dusted their hocks northeast toward Kansas City, yet the expected attack did not come.

"Where the hell are they?" Julius groused when they stopped at a water hole surrounded by dwarf willows.

"It's got me treed," Fargo admitted. "But they sure as hell haven't given up on us. From what I've heard about him, Reed McKinney would rather eat his own guts than give up on a bounty."

"Speaking of eating," Megan complained, "we never did get that hot meal back in Miller's Bend. Skye, you're used to gnawing on jerky for weeks, but I miss real meals."

"Hey, I'd trade a jaw tooth," Fargo assured her, "for a big plate of buckwheat cakes and hot soda biscuits smothered in sausage gravy."

"Don't torture me," Julius begged.

"Anyway, I'm sorry for complaining," Megan told Fargo. "You've put your life on the line to help us. The food is fine."

Fargo sent Megan a long glance as she knelt to splash her face in the water. She reminded him of a bouquet one day after the ball—still quite pretty but starting to wilt from the hardships of a dangerous trail. *This has gone on too long*, Fargo resolved, starting to hatch a new plan.

When the three had finished drinking, filling canteens, and washing up, they led the Ovaro and the palomino forward to drink.

"Why does my horse always hold back until yours has drunk?" Julius asked.

"It's a gelding and he knows mine is a stallion. Horses have a strong pecking order."

"Any settlements at all around here?" Megan asked, gazing out across the flat emptiness.

"A place called Emporia is southeast of us."

"Is it a transportation center?"

Fargo nodded, watching the Ovaro stamp his hooves in irritation at pesky flies. "But I'd rather wear store-bought boots than take a woman into that snake den. We need to fight shy of Emporia. Jayhawkers rule the roost there, not law. I learned my lesson in Miller's Bend."

Fargo felt the palomino for lather. "For a horse carrying two riders, this buttermilk's holding up fine. We've got at least two hours before we have to camp."

They set out again across the flats, Fargo's eagle eyes vigilant. The terrain gradually shifted as they rode through a series of dry washes. Fargo feared ambush and slid his Henry from its boot.

"Skin your shooters," he told the other two.

"Ouch! Watch your damn elbow!" Megan snapped at her father.

"Just how am I supposed to draw my weapon? That gun of yours, by the way, has been poking in my back for hours."

"Then let *me* up front! You—"

"Stow it," Fargo barked. "Both of you. All wrath could come down on us at any moment. Pay attention to things that matter."

However, they negotiated the dry washes and emerged back onto the grassy plain without incident.

"Maybe they've finally given up," Julius suggested. "Megan may be right—could be you hurt 'Bama bad when you took down his horse."

"Anything's possible," Fargo conceded. "I won't count on it, though. After all, *I* walked away from it."

Again Fargo mulled the embryonic plan hatching in his mind—one he hoped to execute this very night. It was either genius or suicidal. *Surprise, mystify, and con-*

fuse, Fargo reminded himself. After all, the only alternative to action was a nameless grave on the prairie.

"Damn it all to hell, anyway!" Reed swore not long after Fargo had fended off their latest attack. "I told you we need help, bo. All we're doing is washing bricks."

He and 'Bama were holding an easy gait, following their quarry at a distance. A homicidal brood had settled over 'Bama, and Reed had eased off him, afraid for his own life. The last time he saw 'Bama in a peeve like this, fresh corpses got stacked up like cordwood.

"I know just the jaspers to help us," Reed said, laying the reins across the right side of his sorrel's neck to head due east. "Emporia ain't but two hours' ride. We'll look up my old pal Nat Bryce. He's the boy for a little sport."

'Bama was silently fuming, and touchy as a sore-tailed grizzly. When Fargo threw his horse, 'Bama had landed on his already wounded shoulder, grinding dirt into it and making it hurt like hell.

"I been keepin' accounts, Reed," he growled. "You hear me? You ain't killin' Fargo, he's *mine*."

"Sure, bo, sure," Reed soothed. "Long as his wick gets snuffed, eh?"

"To hell with Emporia. Let's get Fargo now."

Reed could almost whiff the huge man's rage. 'Bama was slow to rile, but once he did he was hell on two sticks.

"Let's face it, 'Bama. Without help we'll come a cropper one more time. Fargo wasn't born in the woods to be scared by an owl. We need some seasoned fighters. This is the time to go for help—Fargo and the Kinkaids are missing a horse and moving slower. Nat Bryce ramrods a bunch of Jayhawkers now, but I knew him back in the fifties when us two sold Indian burner out in the Bitterroot country."

"I been keepin' accounts," 'Bama repeated with brutal stubbornness, his piglike eyes two pools of burning acid.

Right now everything hung by a thread, and Reed had another source of worry: that damn Cheyenne was still out there, biding his time, watching. As soon as this wide-open terrain closed in, he would strike.

"Get ready for some stink," Reed warned 'Bama.

Another cholera epidemic must have struck
Emporia—a long pesthouse had been erected, west of
town, for the sick and dying. Reed smelled the eye-
watering stench of carbolic acid, used to sanitize the
place.

Like most towns in the Territory, Emporia looked half
built. Several of the dwellings and businesses on the outskirts were simply hides stretched over bent-willow
frames. The two riders reined in at a low cottonwood
log structure with a flap of old hide for a door.

"Now, you just go easy inside there, bo," Reed told
'Bama as they looped their reins around the snortin'
post. "These boys like to cut up rough. It ain't
personal."

'Bama cradled his revolving-barrel scattergun, eyes
burning with the vengeance need. "It's always personal, hoss."

Reed threw back the hide flap, releasing a pungent
cloud of tobacco smoke. After hours in bright sunlight,
he had to let his eyes adjust to the dim interior. About
fifteen men, several sporting plumed hats, were scattered
around the frontier watering hole. Three men armed like
express messengers shared an oilcloth-covered table in
the back corner. They played draw poker in the gutter-
ing light of a candle.

"That's Nat playing poker, the one with the thin Spanish boot dagger," Reed said as he stepped farther into
the room.

Nat Bryce had a face like thirteen miles of bad road
and a disposition to match. He and his band of thirty
Jayhawkers controlled Emporia under the guise of keeping out the proslavery faction. They did indeed kill or
drive out proslavers, but they also lynched blacks.

"Christ, boys!" Bryce shouted. "Look what the cat
drug in! Reed goddamn McKinney and 'Bama Jones!
Look at them sad maps on them two. S'matter, boys,
lose your squaws?"

Laughter exploded in the smoky, sweat-reeking
barroom.

"Easy, 'Bama, go easy," Reed muttered. Aloud he said, "How they hangin', Bryce? Just rode in to see if you're lookin' for a little work."

Shrewdness seeped into Bryce's hard eyes. "Otis," he said to one of the two men playing cards with him, "go have a drink at the bar. I need to reminisce with my old pard."

He kicked two chairs out. "Sit down," he told the new arrivals. "This here is Cas Robinson, my right hand. Cas, these are the famous bounty hunters Reed McKinney and 'Bama Jones. The same boys who roasted all them Cheyenne up near the Republican."

Robinson nodded curtly, staring at both 'Bama's huge stature and his awe-inspiring gun. The Jayhawker was a hatchet-faced man smoking cheap, foul-smelling Mexican tobacco in a corncob pipe.

Bryce passed a bottle of whiskey around. "What kind of work we talkin' about?"

"Me and 'Bama's usual line . . . bounty hunting."

"Well, that ain't *my* usual bailiwick."

"Your part of it is just killing," Reed said. "That's your usual bailiwick."

Bryce's lips twitched into a grin. "Sure is. But your problems ain't none of my funeral."

Reed hadn't seen Bryce in years, and the man had grown insufferable now that he ran his own army.

"I don't like your attitude," Reed said coldly, his cruel mouth set hard.

"You don't have to like it, Reed, but you *will* tolerate it. Look around you."

Reed did. He was known for his fast draw and hair-trigger temper, but among Jayhawkers that cut little ice. No gun-thrower could take on the rifles, shotguns, pistols, revolvers, and knives bristling all over the room.

"All I'm saying," Bryce told his visitor, "is that an empty hand is no lure for a hawk. What's in it for me and my boys?"

"Five thousand dollars," Reed replied, "and free whacks at one fine-looking woman."

Bryce pulled on his chin, considering it. "This woman . . . you say she's prime meat?"

"Right out of the top drawer, bo." Reed fished into

the fob pocket of his leather vest and produced a dodger, unfolding it. "This is a *bad* likeness of her."

Bryce whistled. He was busy building a cigarette. "Yeah, that's mountin' stock, all right. How 'bout the tits? I cannot abide these itty-bitty-titty gals."

"Believe me, Megan Kinkaid is the kind that jiggles when she walks."

"So how many men you need killed?"

"Just one. A drifter that's siding them."

Bryce had been tilting back on the hind legs of his chair. At McKinney's reply, however, he let the chair fall forward with a thump. "One? Ain't this comical, Cas? Big, bad Reed McKinney needs our help to lasso one greasy drifter."

Robinson knocked the dottle out of his pipe, letting some fall on 'Bama's boot. "That's comical, all right. Reed McKinney, pistoleer, hiring out his killing."

McKinney's jaw tightened. "Both you boys are skatin' on thin ice right now."

Bryce sneered. He struck a sulfur match on a front tooth and lit his cigarette. "Do tell? Well, don't let the door hit you where the good Lord split you."

"Ahh, there's good money involved here," Reed surrendered, relaxing.

"That's the gait. So who is this drifter?"

"Skye Fargo."

"Jesus," Robinson cut in. "Ain't he the one they call the Trailsman?"

Reed nodded. Bryce pulled on his chin some more, mulling the proposal.

"This Trailsman," he finally said. "I never met him. But they say he's no boy to trifle with."

"He's been a thorn in my side, sure. But he overrates himself."

"Yeah? Then how come you need my help?" Bryce demanded.

"Because it's time to fish or cut bait. I want this thing over. And I also got a Cheyenne out to lift my dander."

Bryce asked to see the dodger again. "Yes, indeedy, that gal is a huckleberry above a persimmon. And her old man looks like a sister-boy, he'll be no trouble. We can fix Fargo's wagon, all right."

Bryce handed Reed the bottle again. He began paring his fingernails like a rajah at his leisure. "Old son, this is providential. See, me and the boys here are short on cash for fighting the Border Ruffians down in Misery. Might be we can scratch each other's back, hanh? Now, about the skirt—"

"*I* get first whack," Reed insisted. "And I'm bound and determined to hog it at least one whole night. Then it's 'Bama's turn, though he generally passes. After that you boys can hand it around. Just remember, we'll need at least her head to collect the reward on her."

"Fair enough. We'll get the details worked out over some more corpse reviver."

"Nary a peep outside this room," Reed cautioned him. "This is *our* bonanza."

"Don't worry. It stays close to my vest."

'Bama had remained silent since entering. A young Jayhawker at the plank bar called over, "Hey, Jones the Giant! Is that a shotgun or an umbrella stand?"

Laughter spilled through the room. 'Bama looked at the guerrilla and said flatly, "Pups will bark like full-grown dogs."

No threat or challenge was necessary. The danger in his voice, the unmistakable promise of death, sobered the room. Men cleared a ballistics lane, but the offender quickly left.

"And you," 'Bama said, glowing-coal eyes searing into Cas Robinson. "A minute ago you dropped ash on my boot. I been waitin' for you to wipe it off. I ain't waitin' no longer."

Robinson sent his boss an uncertain look, but Bryce gave him a warning shake of the head.

"Sorry 'bout that, 'Bama," Robinson said, hastily dropping to his knees and using his shirttail to clean the boot.

Reed barely controlled his smirk. Good ol' 'Bama, coming through again.

"Best to leave 'Bama alone, boys," he called out. "He's a mite scratchy of late."

16

Toward sundown Fargo called a halt beside a little stream with a sandy bottom. They gave both horses a rubdown, before tethering them in the grass near water, and cooked a hot meal of biscuits and bacon.

"Think McKinney and Jones will come back?" Julius asked around a mouthful of food.

"They're already back," Fargo replied.

Even in the light of the small cooking fire he saw Megan pale. "Where are they?"

"Camped just east of us," Fargo said. "I first spotted them about an hour ago."

"What are they doing?"

"Best I can tell, just watching us."

"That'll change," Julius said bitterly. "That's a cast-iron fact. Get set for a night from hell."

"Yeah," Fargo agreed, recalling his plan from earlier today. "One night from hell, coming right up."

"Why do you think they were gone most of the day, Skye?" Megan asked.

"I hate to say it, but I think they rode into Emporia. The place is infested with Jayhawkers. Could be they cooked up a deal to team up with some of 'em."

"Christ Almighty," Julius swore. "Pile on the agony! As if we don't have enough troubles with the bounty hunters."

"Too many troubles," Fargo agreed, sliding out his Colt. "That's why I'm sneaking into their camp tonight."

"Skye!" Megan exclaimed. "You can't! They'll kill you."

"Distinct possibility," Fargo agreed. "But I learned a

long time ago that you can't let your enemy set the terms of battle. Right now we're just reacting. They decide when to attack, and we beat them back. We need to take the bit in our teeth."

Fargo opened the Colt's loading gate and swung out the wheel, dumping all six bullets into his palm. He blew once to dislodge any blown sand from the cylinders. Then he wiped each bullet clean on his shirt and thumbed them back into the cylinders.

"When you going?" Julius asked.

"Late—just before dawn. That way I'll be here in case they plan to hit us during the night."

"You know I'm good at stealthy movement. I'm also a good shot with a handgun. Want me to come along?"

Fargo shook his head. " 'Preciate the offer, but we can't leave Megan alone." He didn't need to add: *which she will be if we're both killed.*

"Way I see it," Fargo added, "if they do take the risk of attacking us tonight, that means they prob'ly haven't hatched up a plan with Jayhawkers. If they don't attack, that could mean they expect help soon and don't need to risk bracing us on their own. Either way, I need to sneak over."

"Let's all attack their damn camp right now," hot-headed Megan fulminated. "*Now.* I'm not afraid."

Fargo laughed. "I know you're not, firebrand. But *I'm* the biggest toad in this puddle. Sometimes fewer is better. The plan I have in mind works better with one person."

"I wish that Cheyenne would just waltz it to both of them," Julius said.

"He will. But his schedule is different from ours."

He looked at Julius. "I'll be leaving you my Henry. It's fully loaded and there's extra cartridges in my saddlebag. If you can't find targets, make plenty of noise with it."

"Yeah," Julius said with mild sarcasm, "plenty of noise. That'll do it."

Before he rolled into his blanket Fargo spent a long time staring across at the dying fire in the bounty hunters' camp. He got a good fix on locations and distance.

The terrain hereabouts, flat, open, and grassy, both helped and hindered Fargo. It made movement easier, especially for a speedy escape. However, it offered no cover for concealment and protection. Fargo feared the plains more than mountains or forest.

He was leaving his Henry behind to free his hands, which meant the Arkansas toothpick might be even more important to his survival. Fargo slid it from its boot sheath and honed it on a whetstone. Then he settled his head into his saddle and slept like a drugged man, Julius rolling him out for guard well after midnight.

"Any trouble?" Fargo asked as he buckled on his gun belt in the chilly dampness.

"Quiet as a grave," Julius assured him.

Fargo sent him a frowning glance. "Ain't you the sunny one."

"I wouldn't do this, Fargo. Those two are straight from hell."

"That rings right. And high time they were sent *back* to hell."

Fargo took the watch until the glow called false dawn lightened the eastern sky. He woke Megan and Julius, wanting both of them ready in case things went bad at the nearby camp.

Fargo started out across the dark expanse of plain separating the camps. Megan ran to catch up.

"Skye, don't go. We can—"

"Shush it and go back," he told her. "That's an order."

The talking part was over. Now came the hard doing.

Fargo couldn't count on demon drink to make his job easier. Many seedy hardcases on the trail liquored themselves up and passed out drunk in their bedrolls. McKinney and Jones had survived too long, however, to be that careless.

If they were standing watches, Fargo knew his plan was doomed. He didn't think they were—Reed considered himself the big he-dog, so it was others who needed guards. Trusting to this reasoning, Fargo at first moved rapidly closer, using his mind map to stay on a line toward their now invisible camp.

Fargo had made a rough estimate of distance last night, and he counted his strides carefully. It was still night close to the earth, with the sky growing lighter. Fargo's breath ghosted in the crisp, early-morning chill.

When he estimated he'd gone three hundred yards, Fargo slowed to an underwater walk, placing each foot down carefully. He walked on his heels only, to minimize ground contact. As he bent forward to lower his silhouette, he knocked the thong off the hammer of his Colt.

Out ahead, he made out two dark shapes: grazing horses. Fargo had already decided against setting them free, knowing McKinney and Jones would probably murder to get replacements. A moment later one of them caught his scent and whiffled. Fargo froze, right hand palming his Colt.

He heard no one stirring and crept forward, blood pulsing in his temples. Raucous snoring directed his eye to two dark mounds just ahead. Willing himself not to rush out of nervous fear, Fargo selected the obviously bigger mound and slanted toward it.

'Bama Jones snored with a fearful racket like snorting hogs. All of his weapons were laid out beside him in a folded blanket to protect them from dew. Fargo selected the heavy Colt Dragoon with its metal backstrap. Then, carefully, he knelt beside the notorious killer.

Fargo had never descended to murder, not even in clear cases where it was justified for survival. Any man he killed must have a fighting chance, and besides, these two were promised to Shoots Left-handed. So he got a good grip on the Dragoon's muzzle.

With a fluming snort, 'Bama woke up. All at once, wide awake, his rodent eyes burning into Fargo.

"You," 'Bama managed, rising halfway off the ground before Fargo laid the solid butt of the Dragoon into his skull.

The huge man fell heavily to the ground, out cold and wheezing like a leaky bellows. Fargo spun toward Reed, Colt leaping into his fist, but he was still snoring and hadn't missed a beat.

Fargo pulled two strong rawhide thongs from his possibles bag and bound 'Bama's wrists and ankles. He used the man's own bandanna to gag him, then moved to the other side of the cold campfire—Reed's side.

Fargo patiently waited. The sun inched higher, darkness drained from sky and landscape, and when Reed's eyes fluttered open, the muzzle of Fargo's Colt was the first thing he saw. His face froze in terrified fascination, like a bird mesmerized by a snake.

"Looks like you were right, McKinney," Fargo greeted him. "You said the next time you saw me, it would be down a gun barrel."

"The big man," McKinney sneered, his fear suddenly traded for insolence. "Couldn't face me dead on, so he sneaks into my camp like some Digger Indian."

"You just stay right there," Fargo said, wagging the Colt for emphasis. "Something I need to do now that you're awake."

The point of Fargo's plan was to even out the odds. Keeping his gun trained on Reed, he picked up the still unconscious 'Bama's revolving-barrel shotgun. Fargo found a good-sized rock and smashed the workings of the gun.

He returned to Reed. The bounty hunter lay there in silent, impotent rage, stewing in his own juices. Fargo watched him turn his head to study 'Bama's inert form.

"You killed him in his sleep?" he demanded, his tone accusing Fargo.

Fargo laughed. "You hypocritical son of a bitch, you'd gun down a blind man. Don't worry about that mound of garbage, he's alive. Right now, though, he's got less get-up than a gourd vine. Headache, I b'lieve."

Reed had been making it so far on bluff and bluster. Now, however, he seemed to realize he was about to die. His words fairly tumbled over each other in his eagerness to save his bacon. "Fargo, don't jerk that trigger! Me 'n' you can make medicine, anh?"

"Save your breath to cool your coffee," Fargo advised him. "I don't dicker with two-legged roaches who slaughter women and babies."

"Oh, hell, them was flea-bit Cheyenne."

"Women and babies," Fargo repeated. "There's a blood reckoning due on that one."

"All right, Indian lover, kiss my hairy white ass. Why ain't it over by now? I didn't think it was the great Trailsman's style to drag out a killing."

"Speaking of style," Fargo said, almost pleasantly, "they say you like to gut-shoot a man, then finish him with a knife. I like to shoot a man low in the belly, too. Just like I mean to shoot you—low in the belly so you bleed hard inside and die slow."

"Go to hell, crusader," Reed said, though his face had broken out in sweat.

"I've seen it before," Fargo assured him. "You'll lie helpless and screaming for hours, Reed, and you'll bleed so dry you'll *beg* for water. Oh, Christ, you'll beg! You'll burn up with hell thirst at the end, and inside your belly? Why, like jagged glass churning—"

"Put a sock in it!" Reed snapped, his face gone white as milk. "Just jerk the trigger and get it over."

"All right," Fargo agreed. "Strap on your irons."

Reed goggled at him, not understanding. "How's that?"

"I said get heeled. You're hell-bent on seeing me bucked out in smoke. Now's your chance."

McKinney eyed the tall, buckskin-clad frontiersman. Clearly he didn't trust the offer and was searching for the catch.

"This is what you wanted, junior," Fargo assured him. "You been champing at the bit to draw down on me. Now you got your chance."

A wolf grin parted Reed's lips. He grabbed his gun belt, standing up to buckle it on and tie down his holsters.

"Think I'll have this ready, too," he goaded Fargo, sliding the eleven-inch bowie into his belt. "I hate to go back for things. Lead on—we'll both want the sun to our flanks."

Despite Reed's surface bravado, Fargo had noticed a sea change in his manner. He was visibly shaken, and the bully-boy sneer was all show. Fargo kept a careful eye on him as the two men moved out far enough to maneuver out of the sun.

"This was your choice, Fargo," Reed taunted him. "Remember that when you're shoveling coal in hell."

Fargo eyed him, mildly apprehensive but not afraid. The cutaway, tied-down holsters, the rear sights filed off his Navy Colts, and, no doubt, the sear pins filed down so the guns fired at the slightest pressure—all these made a killer but not a man.

"I'm not too worried," Fargo replied as the two men squared off.

"You *ought* to be, buckskins. I'm the best goddamn draw-shoot killer in the country. This ain't the mountain-man West no more, it's a new breed. You've seen your last sunrise, Fargo."

Reed tried to look tough, but Fargo's cold, icy blue stare was unnerving him. The Trailsman saw that and felt gratified—after all, Reed *was* fast—fast as death.

"This ain't my morning to die," he told Reed. "I guess that leaves only you."

"When I finish you off with the bowie, I'm gonna carve a long time."

"Let's get smokin'," Fargo reminded him.

Something in Fargo's tone—the confidence and bravery earned over years of dangerous wandering—seemed to deflate McKinney even more. The hard, cruel mouth trembled to resist panic.

"Satan's waiting," Fargo reminded him softly.

Cursing, Reed went into his slanting crouch, and Fargo watched close, minutely close. Even the best gun-slicks somehow telegraphed their play just before they made it. With Reed, it turned out to be a bunching of the jaw muscles just before he slapped leather.

His right hand moved in a blur of speed, weapon clearing leather just as Fargo's did. Both guns fired as one. Fargo felt a hot wire of pain when the bullet creased his neck. McKinney's screaming reaction, however, startled birds into flight.

His revolver lay where he had tossed it. He hopped around like a man with bees in his pants, blood blossoming from his right hand. "You filthy son of a bitch! You blew off my motherlovin' *thumb*!"

"The cocking thumb of your right hand, to be precise," Fargo clarified. "Like most two-gun toughs, you were only a fast draw with your right hand."

"Bullshit! I'm lightning in both hands."

Fargo palmed the Colt. "Care to demonstrate? I'll bet your left thumb you're lying."

Reed's pain made him lose interest. He went back to howling and dancing, using his shirt to stem the blood. Keeping an eye on him, Fargo headed back to his own camp, feeling satisfied with his plan. That hell-born scattergun was ruined along with Reed's quick-draw threat. And Fargo had kept his word to the Cheyenne.

"Fargo!"

He glanced back. "What?"

"Why didn't you just kill me, you crazy bastard?"

"Because," he replied, "you're promised to someone else who has a better claim."

"Yeah, that's right, you're an Indian lover. That's a gone buck."

"Then it'll be my turn," Fargo reminded him.

"This ain't over, you cockchafer! You hear me? Hell's a-comin' for you! This ain't over!"

"It never is," Fargo said, walking on.

17

"We saw the gunfight, Skye," Megan Kinkaid told Fargo when he'd returned. "And heard those hideous screams. Are you all right?"

"Just hungry, is all. Let's scrape the gravy skillet."

Julius laughed. "Observe the genuine frontier specimen, my dear. Always responding to his most current need. But then, you'd know all about that from experience."

Megan bristled like a feist. "That outrages you, right? Yet, you have no compunction about stealing money and even teaching your daughter to help you?"

Fargo ignored both of them, watching the bounty hunters' camp in the distance. The shotgun was ruined and Reed was in too much pain to make an attack right now. 'Bama, however, would likely recover soon from his conk on the noggin. There was a variety of weapons at his disposal, and Fargo didn't take the big man lightly just because he was stupid—it didn't require brains to be evil and dangerous.

"We heard enough yelling," Julius said, "to know about Reed's thumb. But what happened to 'Bama? Did you kill him?"

Fargo blew on the fire, adding twigs and then sticks they'd been collecting at water holes. "Nah. Just tapped him and tied him up."

Megan suddenly giggled. "I wish I could be there to see it when Reed tackles those knots with only one thumb."

"I like to see you two in good spirits," Fargo told them. "But don't lose sight of the dangers. I'd wager it won't be long before we're being followed by Jayhawkers. Followed teeth to tail."

Megan was filling the coffeepot with water from Fargo's canteen. She paused to stare at him, those big green eyes like bottle glass. "They'll kill you two and rape me. When they've had their use of me, they'll kill me, too. Right?"

"Distinct possibility," Fargo told her. "But if Reed and 'Bama are in the mix, seems likely they'll want . . ."

"First dibs on me?" Megan supplied when Fargo trailed off.

He nodded. "Either way, you'll be dead. Reed prefers to pack a severed head in lime instead of taking prisoners in alive. Saves the price of meals and transportation. We might have to hug with those two again, but our worst enemy right now is Jayhawkers. They'll have the numbers on us."

"And they won't be riding double," Julius tossed in.

"Yeah, that too. Some bands are better than others, but it's best to give them a wide berth. The thing of it is, we're trapped out on the open plains. Now and then there's a fold or gully for cover, but that's about it."

"So what can we do?" Megan fretted.

"What can't be done by dint of sheer force," Fargo replied, "can sometimes be done by wit and wile. You two swindlers ought to know that. We just have to watch for the main chance."

The trio on horseback moved faster, holding a canter and sometimes a lope. The sun tracked higher in a mother-of-pearl sky, and the chilled flesh of dawn was now slick with sweat. Fargo watched the prairie in every direction, still unsure what he would do if he spotted hostile riders. Surrender was certain death, but with three riders on two horses, so was flight.

He reined in at a muddy but safe-looking water hole encircled by several jack pines. Fargo and the Kinkaids drank, filled their canteens, and led the Ovaro and the palomino forward to drink. Still Fargo had seen no sign of pursuers, but he was certain in his heart they would show up loaded for bear.

"How far are we from Kansas City?" Megan asked him as Fargo stretched his back.

"Oh, 'bout two days assuming there's no trouble."

"Wait a minute, I thought you don't make such assumptions," Julius said. "Have you come up with a plan in case we're attacked out here?"

A surge of irritation at Julius and his imperial attitude quickened Fargo's blood. The arrogant little con man needed a few hard slaps. Instead, Fargo removed his hat and whacked at flies with it.

"I've pulled your bacon out of the fire several times by now," Fargo told him. "Maybe *you* oughta come up with a plan. It's your turn."

Megan rolled her eyes. "All he plans are heists."

Fargo waved all this off impatiently. "There is—or was—a little settlement up ahead," he said when they were headed east again. "Johnson City. I had a horseshoe reset there once on my way to the Dakota country."

"Is it really a city?" Megan asked. "You still owe me a dress."

"Not even a town," Fargo assured her. "It'll be awhile before the Plains are really settled. Johnson City, from what I saw, is a headquarters for buffalo hunters, traders, and western emigrants who gave up on the journey to Oregon. Some are the first white homesteaders on the Great Plains, with a good chance they'll all go bust."

"Doesn't sound too promising for our needs," Julius opined. "Do you have friends there who might help us?"

"Not so's you'd notice."

Julius stared at Fargo. "Well, Christ! Is there at least law there?"

"The *least* law, yeah. I seem to recall some old, retired postmaster who was their constable. Mainly he killed stray dogs and recorded property claims that are all illegal anyway since this is all government land."

"And this Johnson City is what you call a plan?" Julius said.

"Never said it was a plan," Fargo corrected him. "But we have to trot before we can canter. Look around you, Kinkaid—endless miles of nothing. If I was you, I'd just pray that Johnson City is still there. It's our only chance."

On the plains, distant objects came into view from the top down as the curve of the earth brought them over the horizon. Fargo had finally spotted the flat roofs of Johnson City when a quick glance over his shoulder revealed a less welcome sight: dust puffs.

"The hounds have our scent," Fargo told the Kinkaids. "Here come the Jayhawkers McKinney sicced on us."

"I can't see anything," Megan said. "How far away are they?"

"Far enough back that we can make Johnson City with an hour or so to spare. Won't even need to chuck up the horses and raise dust of our own."

"Fine," Julius Kinkaid said. "But what's the plan once we *get* to Johnson City?"

"Plans don't come wrapped and ready," Fargo reminded him. "You scratch 'em in the dirt after you see what you've got to work with."

"He got us out of Miller's Bend with just such a plan," Megan reminded her father.

"As to that—he was resourceful, yes, but remember that Skye also dipped into our arsenal. We still have four toss-pots left and two blocks of nitro."

"If it comes down to it," Fargo said, "we'll use toss-pots. *No* nitro within a settlement. We'd blow the whole shebang to smithereens, the guilty and the innocent."

They rode on across the short-grass flats, Johnson City rotating into view only gradually. Fargo's first impression of the place worsened as they rode in on the only street, a wallow of mud and ruts with night slops and animal entrails tossed in for good measure.

Megan's fair oval of a face wrinkled. "My stars! The smell is horrifying."

Few people were out and about on the crude, rammed-earth sidewalks. The usual double handful of buildings were mostly made of cottonwood logs or raw planks. It was one more of those slapdash settlements that, without a river or big stream nearby, would probably not last another five years. Fargo had watched the

120

westering fever sweep the nation since the 1840s, but the movement had plenty of losers and quitters as well as criminals banished from their wagon trains. Many of them ended up in landlocked places like Johnson City.

"You're telling me *this* place will be our salvation?" Julius scoffed. "Fargo, look around you. Only orphans and bachelors would risk this hellhole. There's no place to hide. It's curtains for all of us."

"You go right ahead and bury yourself," Fargo said. "I say, every man to his own gait. But don't bury me. I don't plan on dying today."

One of the log buildings was a saloon with a charcoal-lettered sign calling it the Grizzly's Den. Fargo reined in and looped the Ovaro to the hitching post, loosing the girth and dropping the bridle. Then he unsheathed his Henry.

He pushed open the slab door expecting the usual local hardcases to study them from shadowy pockets of light. But the large, single room with its plank floor and trestle tables was empty of patrons. A few coal-oil lamps spread greasy yellow light around.

"Augh!" growled a voice from behind the bar, a voice like gravel shifting in a rusty hold. "Whoever you are, lower that muzzle. I'll outdrink and outfight any pilgrim half my age! My hand's curled around a hogleg right now, and I can still shoot a squirrel's eye out every pop."

Fargo's face stretched into a grin. He lowered the Henry. "Snowshoe Hendee, you old reprobate. You ain't gone under yet?"

A grizzled old man, still quite spry, hurried out into better light. Snowshoe Hendee had wandered the West most of his life. One-quarter Apache through his dam, he was hawk-nosed, with fierce, dark eyes. He had a wild tangle of frizzled gray hair and a silver beard worn in two braids.

"Well, shit, piss, and corruption! Damn my eyes, it's Skye goldang Fargo! Cut off my legs and call me Shorty! Last time I seen you, colt, was when we wet-nursed them five contract brides out in Hell's Canyon."

"I figured you meant to roost out in the Northwest and run that ferry of yours across the Snake."

"Ah, got the tormentin' itch to move on. For a spell

I went back to the Front Range of the Stony Mountains"—Snowshoe used the old name for the Rockies—"but bilin' mad Injins run me out. I won this roach pit on the third day of a poker game. *Say!* Skye, you been lettin' me cuss a blue streak with a lady present? Sorry, miss, that was just boastful talk about how good I shoot. My cataracts kept me from seein' you."

"Megan Kinkaid, Snowshoe Hendee," Fargo introduced them. "Be vigilant around him, Megan. He's toothless, but he's still got his full quota of original sin."

"Don't be galling me with talk like that," Snowshoe warned, patting the double-bladed throwing hatchet in his sash. "Your topknot will fetch a good price."

Snowshoe's weak eyes raked over Megan at closer range. "Me 'n' the pup here," he told her, ogling openly, "first met down near the Spanish Lake."

"Gulf of Mexico," Fargo translated. "This old fossil uses last century's names."

Julius said, "We happen to be in serious trouble, Mr.—"

"Pah! I know all about your trouble. 'Trouble' is the road me 'n' Skye live on, and bein' on the dodge is old vittles to us. But you? The hell you doin' yondering out here? It's plain from lookin' at you—you're city bred and couldn't locate your own ass at high noon in a hall of mirrors."

"Don't presume on your white hairs, Mr. Hendee."

"I wouldn't threaten him, Julius," Fargo warned. "He's a boaster and a liar, but also tougher than boot leather."

"I won't hurt the little puff," Snowshoe scoffed.

"Besides, Julius is right," Fargo said. "Jayhawkers will be riding in soon looking for us."

"Ain't too surprised. Rumors about you three been thicker than toadstools after a hard rain. Happens you got Nat Bryce on your scent, it's bound to get ugly."

"Nat Bryce . . . don't b'lieve I know the name."

"He ramrods a bunch of Jayhawkers out of Emporia. A ruthless son of a bitch with no soft place in him. Bryce figures life is a disease and the only cure is death. And his *segundo*, Cas Robinson, ain't no better. They got the citizens in this area scared pukey. Word got out they was headed this way—that's how's come there's so few souls stirrin'. C'mere."

Many frontier buildings of that day were equipped with "Indian tunnels" leading from an interior room to a spot well away from the building. Snowshoe led them to a table and dragged it aside. Kneecaps popping like primer caps, he knelt to lift a trapdoor that had been smoothly blended with the raw plank floor.

"Best place to hide," Snowshoe insisted. "They'll have all the buildings searched in jig time. Happens they do find this trapdoor, at least you can fight—maybe even pull foot out the other end. I don't like your chances, though, out on them plains afoot."

"This is a fighting chance," Fargo agreed with his friend. "But we still got the problem of the horses. Our enemies know their color and markings."

"You won't fit *them* in any tunnel," Julius told Fargo. "Short of setting them free, what the hell can we do?"

"Even setting them free wouldn't help," Fargo replied. "Unless they run beyond the horizon, they'd be spotted. No, we'll have to hide 'em best we can. Snowshoe, is there an empty building in town—one without windows?"

The old salt played with his beard braids, thinking. "Matter fact . . . Ben Mumford built an ice house on the edge of town. He plans to harvest winter ice and store it there."

Julius said, "But, Fargo, you heard Mr. Hendee say all the buildings in town can be quickly searched."

"Can be, not *will* be. Snowshoe, grab a white cloth and show us this ice house."

Despite the mounting tension, Fargo had to laugh hard and long when Snowshoe clapped on his conk cover—the old fool had traded his usual beaver hat for the high plug hat of an undertaker.

"Fargo, hell's right under your feet," Snowshoe threatened. "This hat is right fashionable for a man of property like me."

The new arrivals unhitched their horses and quickly watered them at a trough across the street. Then they followed Snowshoe to a low, solid building, the last one on the eastern edge of the rough settlement. The horses

123

shied from the unfamiliar enclosure, and especially the narrow doorway. Eventually, however, they were lured inside by heaps of grain.

"They'll be quiet so long as they're eating," Fargo said. "Then they'll rebel. Let's hope that grain holds out long enough."

"I still don't see how this is smart," Julius complained. "So, fine, the three of us may have a reasonable chance in the tunnel. *Until* the horses are inevitably found."

"They might be," Fargo agreed as everyone stepped outside again. "But don't forget how much this area has been ravaged by plagues. Entire tribes wiped out by yellow fever and cholera. *This* will give them pause."

Julius caught on when Fargo tied the white cloth to the door latch of the ice house—the universal warning that a building was now a pesthouse.

"They might suspect it's bluff," Fargo said. "But it's not rare to see buildings marked for plague. Would *you* take the risk of opening a marked door?"

"Actually, no. There aren't many ways to die more miserably."

"Now you're whistling." Fargo gazed west and saw how the separate dust puffs had formed one boiling, yellow-brown cloud. "We'd best quit jacking our jaws and get into that tunnel—the Jayhawkers are almost here."

18

There was no ladder leading down into the tunnel, so Fargo encircled Megan in both of his arms and lowered her into the dark, cool maw of the entrance.

"Nice set o' lungs on that gal," Snowshoe whispered so only Fargo could hear. The Trailsman winked agreement.

"It's pitch-dark down here," she complained. "What if there are rats? Can't we at least have a stub of candle?"

"Sweet britches," Snowshoe called down to her, "the *dangersome* rats walk on two legs and will be right above you. Glom them big cracks between floorboards—the Jayhawkers might see your light."

"It's not pitch-dark," Fargo assured her. "Your eyes will adjust. Julius, jump down and take my rifle for me."

"Nary a peep," Snowshoe warned them as Fargo lowered himself into the Indian tunnel. "Just stay quiet down there or we'll *all* cop it."

He closed the tunnel entrance, and for a few minutes it was as dark as a coal cellar at midnight. Then, as Fargo's pupils adjusted, he could make out snatches of the barroom through the wide cracks between floor planks.

"Your friend Snowshoe," Megan muttered to Fargo. "I watched him dig a tick out of his scalp. And his smell is . . . indescribable. Does he ever bathe?"

"Never," Fargo assured her. "Not even if he was bunking with the queen of England. He thinks only women and squaw men bother with such things."

"He may smell like a leaking sewer," Julius told his

daughter. "But that scratchy old salt has less fear in him than a rifle. And he's putting his tail in a crack for us."

"You get wiser every day," Fargo told him. "Men like Snowshoe Hendee are the backbone of America. His temper worries me, though. He's got a short fuse."

Megan grabbed Fargo's arm and squeezed it hard when boot heels suddenly thumped over their heads.

"Not yet," Fargo whispered. "The Jayhawkers haven't quite reached town. You'll know when the real fandango's starting."

Fargo glanced through a crack and saw a burly man in hide clothing standing at the bar. Several wolf hides were pressed into a pack he carried under his arm. Wolves were a menace in this area and each pelt was worth a bounty at the county seat.

"Snowshoe!" he hollered, for he was already drunk. "I pine to see my ugly reflection in the bottom of a whiskey glass! Fetch this wolfer a libation."

"H'ar now," Snowshoe growled. "Jimmy lad, 'pears to me you're already out on the roof. Best to get back to your diggin's and get some shut-eye."

"Hookey Walker! This is a dram shop, is it not? Well, dram you, pour it, bottles, *pour* it!"

"Look-a-here," Snowshoe tried to reason. "Jayhawkers are about to swarm Johnson City. This here ain't the best place to be."

"Whiskey, who-shot-John, coffin varnish, corpse reviver, old churnbrain—by any name, I want a bracer! Here, I've planked my cash."

Muttering curses, Snowshoe gave in and thumped a bottle of forty-rod down in front of the insistent customer. Fargo could feel the muffled thunder of approaching riders.

"Be right back," he told the other two. "I'm checking the other end of the tunnel real quick."

Crouched low, using his rifle to feel ahead in the darkness, Fargo quickly reached the end of the tunnel. It simply stopped cold in a pit dug to allow egress. Fargo poked his head up above ground level, squinting in the bright afternoon glare. He had emerged about forty feet due south of the cluster of buildings. The Jayhawkers approached from the west, about fifteen riders.

The tunnel would provide a quick escape at this end, but Fargo gazed around at the endless, flat terrain, devoid of cover, and realized it would only be helpful at night. As he returned to join the Kinkaids, he could only hope the Jayhawkers didn't think to look for a tunnel.

The drunken wolfer at the bar was singing bawdy rhymes about Lu-lu Girl and peeling a boiled egg when the riders reined in out front of the Grizzly's Den with a creaking of leather and clinking of bit rings. Fargo felt the floor vibrate like a drumhead when they came stomping inside, spur wheels chinging.

"Say, dad," rang out a voice of bullying authority, "you must be the *grizzly* in this den, huh?"

Sycophantic laughter filled the barroom. The speaker, Fargo could just make out through a crack, had a thin Spanish dagger tucked in his boot and a face ugly enough to mistake for a bad wound. A hatchet-faced man smoking a corncob pipe hovered near him like a trained toady.

"Must be Nat Bryce and Cas Robinson," Fargo whispered to his companions.

"Who runs this grog shop?" Bryce demanded.

Snowshoe squared his shoulders. "I'm the big bushway here."

"You been here since opening up today?"

"Yep, that I have."

"So you was right here about an hour or so ago?" Bryce pressed.

"Good God, strike a light!" Snowshoe exploded impatiently. "Didn't I just say I was?"

In an eyeblink Cas Robinson's right arm shot over the bar, grabbed the front of Snowshoe's shirt, and yanked his upper body up onto the bar. "Stubborn as a rented mule, huh? Well, *we're* making the medicine, Methuselah, and you're taking it, savvy?"

The Jayhawker slapped Snowshoe hard, several times, each blow making Fargo seethe with rage. He knew his friend's hair-trigger temper and hoped Snowshoe would just play it frosty.

Snowshoe turned choleric with rage but held his tongue.

"Let's start over," Bryce said, reaching over the bar

and passing bottles to his men. "Did three riders, two men and a woman, arrive here in the past hour or so?"

"I heard riders," Snowshoe told him. "I disremember 'zacly how many."

"Didn't they come here?"

Snowshoe shook his grizzled head. "Nope."

"Did they ride *into* town or around it?"

"Most likely they went around, happens there was a female with 'em. Most women won't go into saloons like this, and we got no eating houses in Johnson City."

Fargo watched Bryce stare at Snowshoe, trying to decide if he was lying.

"Pete, Sparky, Corey!" he barked out. "Search every building. *They* might be able to hide, but a horse don't fit under a bed."

Bryce slid the dagger from his boot and brought the point under Snowshoe's nose. "I find out you're lying, old man, I'll carve out your heart and feed it to your asshole."

"Huh," Snowshoe said, subdued but not quailing. "No need to come in here bawling like a bay steer. I told yous, I ain't seed hide nor hair of 'em."

Fargo had been worried about the drunk wolfer, who had wisely stayed out of things so far. Now, however, whiskey fumes made him push into it.

"This is mighty high-handed behavior, boys," he announced with the exaggerated solemnity of drunks. "You Jayhawkers ain't the law."

"No," Cas Robinson agreed. "Here's the law."

The explosion, in that small building, was deafening when a double load of eighteen buckshot from a Wells-Fargo gun tore Jimmy nearly in half. Robinson broke open the gun, slid shells into the twin chambers, and swung the still-smoking weapon toward an ashen-faced Snowshoe. "Now if *you're* feelin' froggy, old codger, go ahead and jump."

Megan began quietly sobbing while Fargo's reaction was pure, white-hot anger. And guilt—true, the wolfer's lack of good sense and sobriety got him killed, but Fargo and the Kinkaids had drawn these pitiless murderers to Johnson City.

There was even more to worry about if the pesthouse

ruse didn't work. Once those horses were discovered, the Jayhawkers would encamp here. They would also realize tunnels were in the mix and search for them. Nor, without horses, could Fargo and his charges ever hope to escape.

However, Lady Luck finally chose to smile on them.

"Whole town's clean, Nat," called one of the Jayhawkers as the three returned from their search. "No sign of them or their mounts."

"That was *every* building?" Bryce demanded.

"Yep. Top to bottom."

Fargo allowed himself a brief grin. With the predictable self-preservation of lower-ranking vigilantes, Bryce's men had lied rather than search a potential pesthouse. Most men gave them wide berth, afraid they infected the surrounding air with pestilence, creating a miasma or poison gas.

"Looks like they rode on past," Bryce said to Robinson and his men. "You were right; they've lit a shuck toward Kansas City. Don't matter, we'll catch up. They got two days of naked plains to cover on two horses. We got Fargo's dingus in a wringer, chappies, and we're gonna *squeeeze*."

"You three hang on a bit," Snowshoe called as the thuggish militia rode out. "Might be a fox play."

Snowshoe finally pronounced the Jayhawkers in genuine flight to the east. Fargo pulled himself out and helped the others up. He and Snowshoe gazed on the mangled body of the wolfer until Snowshoe covered it with a Navajo blanket.

They dug a simple grave near a dozen others out on the nearby prairie. The body was wrapped in the blanket and tied with two ropes. Snowshoe burned gunpowder over it to discourage predators.

"I'll put a marker on it tomorrow," he said. "For right now, you three follow me."

Rumors about Jayhawkers had kept Johnson City swept of people, and Snowshoe didn't bother with locking up his grog shop. He led them to a partially enclosed stock shelter used by the entire settlement.

"Skye tells me you're shy one horse," Snowshoe said

to Megan. "Take thissen. Any friend of Skye Fargo's is kin to me."

All three of them gaped in astonishment when Snowshoe handed her the bridle reins of a pretty little strawberry roan.

"She's lady-broke," Snowshoe explained. "Only four years old. A little prettier than I like in a horse, but this little mare has plenty of bottom. And she's bullet-wise, too. You'll need that, ridin' with Skye."

"Oh, Mr. Hendee, *thank* you. But we have no money—"

"Didn't cost me one red cent, missy. Won her in a poker game, too, just like I done the saloon and wagon."

Fargo watched Julius perk up. "Sounds like you dabble in games of chance?" the grifter remarked casually.

Snowshoe's wrinkled face turned crafty. " 'At's right, pilgrim. Fancy yourself a gambler, do you?"

"Snowshoe," Fargo warned, "if I were you—"

"Whack the cork, infant," Snowshoe whispered. "I'll carve this *perfumado* a new one."

"All right," Fargo gave in. "Like you said, you're the big bushway."

"*Augh!* Damn right I am." Snowshoe, still watching Julius from cunning eyes, said, "You three can't leave so soon behind them killers. Rest your horses, eat, grab a few hours' shut-eye on something besides ground. Mebbe me 'n' you, Mr. Kinkaid, could have us a friendly session of draw poker?"

"Well, they do say that no man ignorant of cards need bother going west," Julius replied. "Perhaps a few rounds of poker."

"A few *hands*," Snowshoe corrected him, winking at Fargo. That wink said *easy pickings*.

The warm sun was westering. They began walking back toward the saloon, Megan leading the strawberry. All three horses were soon staked in the grass behind the Grizzly's Den.

"Ain't no hotel in this flea pit," Snowshoe explained, pointing to an old prairie schooner parked near the back door of his saloon. Its covering canvas was still sturdy. "So I rent out beds in that. Eiderdown quilts and feather pillows, even. Room for all three of you in there."

"Is there any place around here to take a bath, Mr. Hendee?" Megan asked.

Snowshoe looked surprised. "Bath? You? Darlin', you smell fresh as a mountain mornin'. C'mere."

Snowshoe took them inside the back room, which had been made into a bathhouse of sorts. There were a mirror and washstand, a small woodstove with a tin pipe chimney, and a big metal tub.

"Well's right outside," the old-timer told her. "You can heat the water on the stove if you've a mind to. Don't worry none about privacy. Ain't no door but this back one, and it bars tight from the inside."

"I'll get a fire going in here," Fargo volunteered, for as sundown approached the air was growing crisp.

"Now, pilgrim," Snowshoe said, tugging on his beard braid as he studied Julius from calculating eyes, "what say me 'n' you buck the tiger? I got a clean deck out front."

Fargo bit his lip to keep from laughing when Julius again looked hesitant. "Well, just a few rounds . . ."

"Hands," Snowshoe corrected with a chuckle, winking at Fargo. "*Hands.*"

The two men moved around front while Fargo set kindling ablaze and tossed a few stove-lengths onto the fire. As he was heating buckets of water and pouring them into the tub, Megan peeled off dress, petticoats, and pantaloons. She undid her chignon, letting wheat-blond tresses tumble over her back and shoulders like a golden waterfall.

Fargo, feasting his eyes on the sight, then reluctantly started to leave so she could have her bath.

"Skye?"

He turned around, not bothering to hide the tent in his trousers. "Yeah?"

"I've read that bathtubs are carriers of diseases, especially when filled with hot water. So . . ." She lifted both breasts as if offering them to him. "Let's get sick together."

Fargo grinned and dropped the bar across the door. "Good idea. I won't have to fill another tub."

Fargo stripped buck and set his weapons within reach. Then he eased into the hot water with her, fully aroused.

131

"My goodness," she giggled, one hand wrapping his manhood. "It pokes way out of the water like a lighthouse. Here, let me scrub it."

Pleasure jolted Fargo from scalp to toes when she wrapped a washcloth around his hard length and began gently rubbing it. A tight, tickling, warm, throbbing sensation pulsed from his shaft down to his groin as she increased the pressure and tempo of her strokes.

"Oh, it's getting hard as steel," she breathed excitedly, her breath warm and moist in his ear. "We won't waste this one!"

She rose to her knees, cocked one leg, and straddled Fargo, using one hand to line them up as she plunged down onto him, gasping at the sensation.

"Oh, *my!*" she exclaimed, hips gyrating faster and faster. "That is *so* nice!"

Fargo could only agree as he lay back in the tub and let this delightful demon do all the work. Faster, harder, she pistoned up and down, squeezing him from the base of his shaft to the very tip. Water began to splash, then slosh, out of the tub, which eventually began to rock as Megan, keening with primitive pleasure, drove both of them over the precipice.

"*Now,* Skye!" she gasped, flopping like a rag doll as a powerful climax exploded through her. Fargo almost bucked her out of the tub when his own release made him arc like a taut bow.

Neither one of them moved for several minutes, depleted by their spent lust. Then they both quickly finished their baths.

Fargo dressed, then threw the bar off the door and nudged it open. "It's sundown now. I hate like hell for us to ride after dark—increases the chances of laming a horse. But we better at least get well clear of town before we camp. We'll have to take a less direct route toward Kansas City so we'll miss the returning Jayhawkers."

"Skye," she called as he started to head out, "what about McKinney and Jones? Will they be after us again?"

"Hard to call. Reed's got a wound that could infect and kill him within days. If he's able to treat it, yeah, we could still have those two thorns to remove. But don't forget, he's lost his quick-draw hand and there's a Cheyenne brave looking to lift his hair."

Around front, Fargo found the poker game about as he'd expected. Julius, who couldn't have had much stake money to begin with, now had an impressive pile of gold and silver coins in front of him. Snowshoe looked more battle-shocked than angry.

Fargo said, "We're heading out. Our friends could be back anytime. Snowshoe, just stick to the story you gave them earlier, and *don't* give them the rough side of your tongue. They can't prove we were here or that you helped us."

Snowshoe disappeared and Julius turned his gaze on Fargo. "Plenty of noise from that back room," he remarked. "I've never heard a bathtub rocking before."

"That was me kicking on the stove," Fargo lied.

"The stove must have liked it, then, judging from the encouragement it was giving you."

Fargo left that one alone. He and Julius played a few hands of draw poker until Snowshoe returned fifteen minutes later with a bundle of roast-beef sandwiches wrapped in cheesecloth.

"For the trail," he told them. "And le'me give you some advice about Jayhawkers—just like with Comanches, *never* surrender. The dying is ten times harder. Keep one bullet in reserve for yourself."

19

Night deepened and an endless profusion of stars took over the blue-black dome of sky. Fargo still believed the Jayhawkers would return to Johnson City after failing to cut sign on their quarry, so he and the Kinkaids were riding at an oblique angle toward Kansas City, leaving the more direct trail to the Jayhawkers.

Fargo's plan for avoidance was necessarily simple, given the stark reality of the terrain. They would out-flank the returning Jayhawkers on their right, or north, side, jutting a few miles due north. Then Fargo's group would cut east again to sweep around the enemy toward Kansas City.

"How's that strawberry?" he asked Megan.

"Wonderful, so far. She responds well to the bit and has a very comfortable gait."

"She 'pears to have plenty of bottom, too," Fargo said. "That'll come in handy if we have to run."

"You think we'll be having a set-to with the Jayhawkers, don't you?" Julius asked Fargo.

"Don't know about us," he replied, "but *I* will be."

"Why?" both Kinkaids demanded at once.

For a moment Fargo recalled the obscene, liquid-slapping sound of Jimmy Boyda's blood coming through the floorboards. Nor would Fargo forget the way Cas Robinson had smacked Snowshoe around.

"Because it's a debt owed to Snowshoe and Johnson City," he replied. "We lured the trouble there. Now I have to somehow keep the Jayhawkers from riding back—draw them off somehow."

A coyote howled, the sound trailing off into a long, yipping bark.

"Isn't this too far east for coyotes?" Julius asked.

"I'd say so," Fargo replied, loosening his Henry in its boot. "They don't migrate much, but it's close to a drought in the Southwest."

"Skye, how would you draw the Jayhawkers off?" Megan pressed him.

"Well, the main point is to show myself so they know I'm not holed up back in Johnson City. Then I'll have to shake 'em somehow."

"Don't forget," Julius chimed in, "there's four toss-pots left."

Fargo stroked his chin whiskers, mulling it. "You know, a few toss-pots just might unnerve this bunch, at that. It's a lot of smoke and noise, and that'll spook their horses. But as killing bombs they're pretty puny."

"Which means," Julius said, taking up Fargo's thread of thought, "after the Jayhawkers get scared, they'll get mad."

"And then we'll need something more convincing," Fargo said.

Megan glanced over at him. "But I thought you were opposed to using the nitroglycerin?"

"In town, hell yes. One pound of nitro leaves a crater the size of an opera house. Out here, though, it's just dirt and sky. Let 'er rip."

Megan exchanged a quick glance with her father. "But Skye, that nitro—"

"Never mind the nitro for now," her father cut in. "We may not have to use it."

Fargo gauged the time by the color of the moon and the position of the polestar. Soon it would be time for him and Julius to cut south and see if they could intercept Nat Bryce and his criminal army. Fargo tried to ignore the words nagging at him, advice he always tried to follow until he met these grifters: *poke not fire with a sword.*

Shoots Left-handed slid the hair bridle off his pony and tossed aside the flat, buffalo-hide saddle. Working quickly before the night wind chilled his mount, he wiped him vigorously with a blanket stolen from the blue-bloused soldiers.

The cold moons were coming. Soon his tribe would pack the entire camp on travois and move south to a winter site. He missed his parents and the rest of his clan, missed the comfort and routine of camp life. This terrible matter had dragged on too long, but finally the Cheyenne subchief sensed the end to this long and bloody drama was at hand. Forces had been set in motion and now the rulers of the cardinal points would shape destinies.

Shoots Left-handed, calling on the legendary horsemanship of the Cheyenne, had hovered on the horizon lines to watch events unfold earlier. Most of all he was watching the *mah-ish-ta-shee-da* devils who had slaughtered his people. Clearly, although Shoots Left-handed did not see it happen, they had tangled with the man whites called Fargo. Perhaps Fargo had kept his word that he would try not to kill them—the smaller bounty hunter with the two guns on his belt now wore a bloody cloth tied around his right hand.

More important to the Cheyenne, that big-talking gun was gone. The same gun that recently killed he who must not be mentioned. Nonetheless, it was terrain that dictated battles, and Shoots Left-handed now had a sacred duty that was more important than dying gloriously.

With those two butchers, in open plains like this, he would have only one chance to close for the kill. It must be carefully selected. His own death was not the main consideration. The rigid code of the Cheyenne warrior was etched in his mind and heart: bear pain in silence, meet death with defiance. But Shoots Left-handed feared that, if he was killed, these men would leave this region and return to a place east of Great Waters, where Cheyenne couldn't find them. That left the Medicine Arrows stained with blood and ensured the suffering and demise of his people.

All day long the butchers had slowed down, seeming content to wait while the war party of *mah-ish-ta-shee-da* criminals went after Son of Light and the oddly dressed man and woman. Devils on every side. Shoots

Left-handed admired the lone hero in buckskins and did not want the bounty hunters or these new killers to send him under. Better that, however, than allowing him to kill the two white butchers before a Cheyenne could.

So now was the time to finally bridge the gap. However, Shoots Left-handed would not repeat the mistake made by he who must not be named. Most Cheyenne braves would run away from a battle, with no loss of honor, if they had not first danced and painted. The hot-tempered one who died had attacked the butchers without doing either.

While Uncle Moon shaded from white to yellow, Shoots Left-handed made his clay-painted face gruesomely magnificent: forehead yellow, nose red, chin black. He donned his single-horned warbonnet, its tail long with coup feathers. Then, forgetting the stream of conscious time, he danced until the trance glaze was over his eyes. And with the trance—a serene bravery in the face of any suffering—he was ready to meet the enemy in a fight to the death.

"Fargo got lucky when he crippled my hand, bo," Reed McKinney repeated for at least the dozenth time that day, his voice raw-edged with bitter hatred. "But that meddling bastard is shit out of luck now, anh? We'll flush him out quick."

He and 'Bama were well east of Johnson City, following the path of the Jayhawkers. Reed kept the horses' gait to a slow trot to ease the fiery jolting in his right hand. The thumb had been severed cleanly at the second joint, and Reed had buried it with tears in his eyes. With that thumb he could have entered the pages of history; without it he would become just another pissant drone leading an unchronicled existence.

"No more attempts on our own," Reed cautioned 'Bama. "I can't draw or shoot fast, and your smoke pole is gone. Not to mention we got a pissed-off Cheyenne doggin' us. We'll join up with Nat, safety in numbers."

"Won't be no *attempt*, hoss—you got that right," 'Bama replied. "That son of a bitch ruint my favorite gun! But I still got my big Colt Dragoon, and I mean to shoot that bastard to tripes."

"Yeah? Well, you can get in line, bo. It won't be no draw-shoot, but I still got a left thumb to cock with. Hey, I won't kill him right off, that's too merciful. I'm puttin' a bullet or two into his spine, then slicing open his voice box. That way, buzzards and wolves will eat the son of a bitch alive, and he won't even be able to twitch or yell. I—"

Reed paused in his ranting to peer out ahead across the moonlit plains. Shadowy riders appeared against the night sky, plenty of them.

"Nat's bunch," Reed said, sinking steel into his sorrel. "They're heading back. Musta already caught Fargo and the Kinkaids. C'mon, bo, time to settle some accounts."

20

Fargo and Julius divided up the toss-pots, each taking two in his saddlebags. The three riders had halted in a small depression that would offer Megan some concealment while she waited for the men to return.

"Keep your horse tacked and hobbled next to you," Fargo instructed. "If you hear anything, more than two riders coming in, hit leather and ride hard in this direction."

Fargo consulted the sky, then used his Arkansas toothpick to carve a line in the sod, its arrowhead tip pointing due east. "That's the direction to Kansas City. See that bright star burning low? That's the dawn star. Keep it straight out in front of you. Is your gun loaded?"

Megan nodded. "Five bullets for the Jayhawkers, one for me. You're right, Skye, there's things worse than death."

"If you get into a shooting scrape," he asked, "you gonna waste time aiming?"

She smiled. "Nope. Just point and shoot, like the gun is an extension of my finger."

"Atta girl." Fargo admired her sand and regretted leaving the beauty alone to fend for herself. However, he was duty-bound to protect Snowshoe and Johnson City.

"Your dad and me will return," Fargo assured her. "But be ready to ride—we'll likely have vigilantes nipping at our heels."

That was the trickiest part of Fargo's plan—by showing themselves and detonating the toss-pots, he and Julius would draw the Jayhawkers away from their return to Johnson City. However, the two men had to ensure they opened enough of a lead to pick up Megan and then stay ahead of the Jayhawkers until at least dawn. Fargo would need some light to find a spot where the nitro blocks could be effectively used.

"Question," Julius said as the two men rode out toward the south. "How do you know when and where the Jayhawkers will turn back? Or even *if*?"

"The same way you know when to palm an ace or sneak into a vault—experience. They've likely turned back by now. In fact . . ."

Fargo reined in and swung down from the saddle, landing light as a cat. A vagrant wind gust brought him the sound of bits and spurs clinking. He dropped to one knee and felt the ground with his fingertips.

"They're out there," he announced. "Still riding hard, too. That's good news for us. Means their mounts should be tired."

Fargo lay down flat on his stomach and studied the vast darkness ahead. The sky was a shade or two lighter than the ground, and soon he spotted vague shapes bobbing just to their east.

"Think I got a bead on them," Fargo said. "C'mon, let's put at 'em."

"You know," Julius said nervously, "these toss-pots only have six-second fuses. And these men are riding hard. It's not like we can just light them and run."

"Won't need to," Fargo assured him. "The Jayhawkers won't be bothering with outriders for security, not against just three of us. Hard as they're riding they won't hear two more horses joining the rear. We'll have to work fast, though. And we'll need these."

Fargo slid the Arkansas toothpick from its boot sheath and cut two pieces off the rope coiled around his saddle horn. He struck a lucifer to life with his thumbnail and set one end of each piece glowing.

"Matches are the dickens to light at a lively gait," he told Julius. "Just let the rope dangle, breeze will keep it smoldering. Throw your bombs up into the middle of the formation, then light a shuck due north. C'mon, let's loop around and swing in behind 'em."

"Hell," said a skeptical Julius, "why not just *fly* over them and drop the toss-pots? Fargo, I fear I used up my quota of good luck when we shot our way out of Miller's Bend."

"Nerve up," Fargo told him. "They won't be looking for us to infiltrate their own ranks. These Indian tactics got their points. Besides, worst they can do is kill us."

It was tricky, nerve-rattling work. Fargo and Julius Kinkaid loped their horses in a curving pattern, staying just out of sight of the riders and finally coming up behind them.

Fargo's experience proved right. With fifteen horses thundering over the plains, two more could ease up close. He and Julius worked together, timing everything carefully. They each pulled a toss-pot from a saddlebag, lit the fuse with their burning ropes, then lobbed the bombs toward the center of the tight formation.

KA-WHUMPF!

Dirt slapped Fargo's face hard as the two toss-pots exploded as one, lighting up the night and showing a portrait of chaos from the brush of a demented artist. Several horses went down, tossing their riders and causing a massive pileup. Men flew into the night sky, britches burning, screaming in fright.

However, the Ovaro and the palomino, too, were spooked by the deafening explosion and blinding light. The Ovaro chinned the moon and almost sent Fargo hurtling backward over the cantle. He was still fighting to calm the stallion when a voice near the back of the chaotic formation shouted, "Eyes to the rear, boys! *Son of a bitch*, it's Fargo and Kinkaid!"

Still barely in control of his horse, Fargo spotted the speaker just as the man raised a six-shooter and began blazing away at him. The Trailsman jerked his Colt and felt it buck in his fist. The thug folded to the ground like an empty sack, but the damage had been done. Several men were chucking hot lead at the two intruders.

"No time to toss the second one!" Fargo shouted to Julius above the din of gunfire. "Let's vamoose!"

Fargo calmed the Ovaro and tore off to the north, a racket of gunshots behind them. He cursed at their inability to toss those second bombs. They would have killed or wounded more horses and men, and created greater shock. That was crucial to opening out an adequate lead and, thus, having time to find a good defensive position. As things stood now, several riders were already pounding after them.

Rounds flew in nineteen to the dozen, and Fargo felt a sharp tug when one passed through his buckskin trousers. Moments later another round *flumped* into his blanket roll, and Fargo suddenly got mad. These murdering sons of bitches knew only one form of authority.

Fargo braced one hand on his pommel, the other on his cantle, and lifted himself from the saddle, spinning around and seating himself again in the opposite direction. The well-trained Ovaro kept galloping as Fargo speared the Henry from its boot and opened fire on the pursuers, raining lead on them. One of the men was wiped from the saddle when a round caught him in his lights.

Seconds later, fizzing sparks arced through the night when Julius threw his second toss-pot. Fargo watched it land just in front of the lead pursuers. Instead of exploding, the defective weapon turned in a rolling, bouncing, sputtering fountain of brilliant red-and-orange sparks as the powder burned itself out.

Fargo, so entranced he stayed backward in the saddle to watch it, realized the dud was a godsend. All three lead horses, and more behind them, panicked at the fiery display and bolted.

He spun back around, kicked his feet into the stirrups, and took up the reins.

"Sharp piece of work!" he shouted to Julius. "Damn straight they saw both of us. We whittled 'em down a little, but there's still too many. These boys nurse a grudge, and they *will* come after us. Right now we have to get to Megan before they do."

The two riders reached Megan without incident, and all three were headed east toward Kansas City, still about thirty hours riding time away, by Fargo's estimate, when dawn finally broke.

"Still behind us?" a weary Megan asked, slapping dust off her bodice.

"Not only still behind us," Fargo reported as he stood up from his latest ground check, "but growing in numbers. Bryce must have reserves around here."

"How close are they?" Julius asked.

"Hard to say. A few hours at the most, an hour at the least. And I still don't see anything but flat. We need some little piece of high ground or they'll cut us down like wheat."

Fargo stepped up into leather, feeling the Ovaro's lathered neck. All three horses had seen hard service lately, and more was looming.

They moved on at a lope, Megan's roan mare and Fargo's stallion naturally staying close.

"What in blazes is that?" Julius demanded, pointing south.

Fargo had already spotted, well across the plains, two mobile wagons loaded with equipment for the Beardslee Flying Telegraph.

"It's a portable telegraph."

"Soldiers?" Megan asked.

"Could be," Fargo told her. "Or railroad surveyors. There's troops in this area, so the workers can call for help if Indians or ruffians threaten them."

"Well, *we* have ruffians threatening us," Megan said. "Can't we call for help?"

Julius laughed. "Give the child her pacifier. Megan, your pretty face can't paper over the facts. All three of us are wanted criminals, and these army chaps have all the latest reward dodgers. We'll have to get out of this on our own."

" 'Fraid so," Fargo agreed. "With, maybe, a little help from those nitro blocks. Actually, a *lot* of help."

Megan stared daggers at her father, who rode to the left of Fargo. "You said you were going to tell Skye. Obviously you didn't."

"Tell me what?" Fargo demanded.

"It's nothing," Julius evaded, suddenly interested in the new sun and the sneeze-bright morning.

"Yes, it is," Megan told Fargo. "When Father robbed the arsenal, he took toss-pots because they were stable to transport. But the nitroglycerin blocks scared him. So he took two that had been tagged 'expired munitions.' He took the tags off, meaning to sell the nitro to cracksmen as still potent."

Fargo did a slow boil. "So it's all just another con? You think we can stop ruthless murderers with worthless nitro? Just *miracle* their asses into hell?"

"Didn't think you intended to use it," Julius replied. "You raked me over the coals for having it."

Fargo sighed. "That I did, didn't I? Anyhow, it's past talk now, I s'pose. The army makes plenty of mistakes, and it's hard to judge when explosives are too old. That nitro might still have some kick."

Fargo sure-god hoped so, anyhow. Because these horses were losing bottom and the terrain still offered no defensive position. Which meant, when the final clash came, there would be no time for niceties such as breastworks, rifle pits, or pointed stakes.

"We've still got one toss-pot," Julius reminded him, pretending this pathetic fact was a silver lining.

"Yeah," Fargo said, fixing a steely blue stare on the grifter. "And I know right where I'm tempted to toss it."

21

By an hour after sunrise, the horses were blowing hard.
Fargo was forced to order that all three riders dismount
and walk their horses for ten minutes each hour. He
could see the Jayhawkers behind them, an indistinct blur
that was slowly gaining.

"Almost time to make a stand," he told the Kinkaids.
Both looked weary and scared, but still determined to
survive. "The horses are done in, and we'll never reach
Kansas City before those prairie rats overtake us."

"Don't we need high ground, like you said?" Megan
asked.

Fargo nodded. "We can't see it yet because the Republican River is ahead of us. There's folds in the
ground that block our view. Should be high ground
ahead—I once scouted along this stretch of the river."

The riders slowed to a trot for the next half hour. All
weapons had been reloaded before Fargo and his
charges took a little nourishment in the saddle.

"Look!" Megan exclaimed, pointing northwest. "It's
that Cheyenne, I think. What's he doing?"

Fargo had spotted Shoots Left-handed ten minutes
earlier. "Indians are notional, so it's hard to know for
sure. I'd say he just wants to know where I am."

"Oh, that's right. He's afraid you might kill the bounty
hunters before he can."

"Real afraid," Fargo said. "Him being this close tells
me McKinney and Jones are with the Jayhawkers by
now."

"That caps the climax," Julius lamented.

"No, for us it's good news," Fargo assured him. "Best to keep your enemies close and in one place."

"Skye, I can make out individual riders behind us," Megan fretted. "Until now they were one mass."

"Buck up," Fargo told her. "See that ridge just ahead?"

"It's not much of a ridge," Megan said uncertainly. "Is it?"

"It's a puny showing," Fargo admitted. "Too low for my liking. But it's got those long, sloping sides with that stand of pine trees."

"Wind-twisted pine trees," Julius corrected him. "A man would have to be a contortionist to hide behind them."

"Julius, you are one sunny bastard," Fargo said. "By your reckoning, us three are already dead."

He watched Shoots Left-handed fade to the north as the Jayhawkers drew ever closer—faster than the ridge seemed to.

"Fargo!" a nervous Julius called out. "Still plan on trying the expired nitro blocks?"

"We have to. We can't shoot our way out of this one."

"I don't exactly know how to use it," Julius admitted.

"There's a well on top of the block for a blasting cap. You just crimp the fuse to it. But we got a problem besides the old nitro—the fuse packed in with the nitro is supposed to burn between thirty and forty-five seconds per foot. But the black powder in it gets dry over time, and the damn thing might ignite in three seconds. I've seen it happen."

"So what can we do?" Megan implored.

"Try to detonate the nitro blocks with bullets," Fargo replied. "Using fuses is foolish in our case. The Jayhawkers would see us lighting them. This way we can hide the blocks in strategic locations and not give them away."

They finally reached the grassy slope leading to a ridge overlooking the banks of the Republican. Even as they gained the ridge, Fargo saw a spearhead of five riders leave the formation to attack first.

"Horses hobbled in the pines!" Fargo barked. "Then lie down flat behind a tree. They'll have ammo to waste, but we save ours for sure targets. I'll be right back."

Fargo hurried to the palomino and pulled the nitro blocks from the hidebound bag. The five riders were pounding closer, so Fargo raced down the slope, hoping they couldn't see the nitro before he planted it. One block he tucked behind a rock, hidden to those approaching but visible from the pines. The other he took farther downslope, where he scooped out a hole for it.

"What do you do, Fargo," he muttered, "when this useless shit fails you?"

He was nearly back up the slope when the spearhead, evidently sharpshooters, opened up on him. Bullets chased his heels the rest of the way up, then began hissing and cracking into the pines.

"Hold your fire!" Fargo shouted when Julius began to aim.

"Why aren't *you* shooting?" the grifter demanded above the sound of gunfire below them. "They're in range of your rifle!"

"Settle down," Fargo told him. "This is just a softening attack. The real push comes next, and we'll want all our ammo. We don't even know if that nitro will work, so we have to fight as if we don't even have it."

A bullet tore loose a chunk of bark and sent it spinning into Fargo's face. He levered the Henry and dropped a bead on one of the five point riders as he began to surge up the slope. The Henry thumped into Fargo's shoulder, and the Jayhawker's face disappeared in a red smear.

"Good work, Fargo!" Julius congratulated. "The other four are leaving."

"Yeah, but we won't like what's coming."

"Look!" Megan cried. "There's Reed McKinney riding close to the man who murdered the hider in Johnson City."

"Cas Robinson," Fargo supplied the name. "And 'Bama just behind them. That's Nat Bryce leading the main charge."

Fargo weighed the decision to conserve ammo against the need to prevent a full-bore charge up the slope. He estimated nearly twenty men coming at them. If they overran this position, it would get ugly in a hurry.

"We need to stop them farther out," Fargo decided,

tossing the butt of the Henry into his shoulder socket. "Here goes!"

Again and again Fargo levered and fired, the stock slapping his cheek as he sent lead humming below. The man to Bryce's left caught a bullet in his throat and flew off his horse, only to be trampled by the riders behind him. A second man was wounded in the elbow and sent up hideous, unnerving screams. The charge was broken.

"Why aren't they firing back?" Julius wondered.

"The leaders of the Jayhawkers generally have military training," Fargo replied. "A storm of lead is coming. You two hunker down."

Proving Fargo right, Bryce snapped commands that brought all of his riders into a line about two hundred yards out.

"Press down flat," Fargo warned again. "And *don't* raise your head."

"Full front face!" Bryce shouted. "Fire!"

Fargo had been trapped before under massed enfilade fire, but this surpassed any in ferocity. He made himself as flat as possible, trying to get his wide shoulders behind a skinny tree. Bark, pine needles, grass, and dirt filled the air as hundreds of slugs hurtled in at them. The crackle of rifles firing made one continuous sound.

"Jesus, Fargo," a frightened Julius said during a brief lull as the vigilantes reloaded, "what if they charge again? Are you going to try the nitro?"

"Has to be done at the right moment," Fargo told him. "But don't count on it to blow. If they make it up here, retreat along the ridge and use tree cover. Don't waste a shot. *Look out!*"

The next volley of shots ripped into their position like destructive fangs, shredding, chewing, ripping. The horses neighed loudly, severely frightened. In the midst of the din, Fargo suspected they were using the Beardslee Flying Telegraph to send for help. He knew, however, that it was way too late for anyone to save them. They'd either paddle their own canoe or sink.

"Charge!" Nat Bryce roared, and a full-throated yell went up from his cutthroat army.

Fargo cursed. He had been forced to expend most of

the Henry's remaining rounds to break the first charge. Now he needed to save what he had left for an attempt to detonate the nitro—he didn't trust his aim, at this distance, with his Colt.

Several riders gained the slope before the main body. One was Cas Robinson, sporting the same Wells-Fargo gun that had torn Jimmy, the wolf hunter, in half. He headed his galloping horse straight at Fargo, eyes crazy with bloodlust, screaming at the top of his lungs.

Blood surged into Fargo's face and he rolled fast to one side right as the express gun went off, scooping out a trench where Fargo had just lain. The Trailsman groped for his right boot, rocked up onto his knees, and threw his Arkansas toothpick with all his strength. The long, thin knife sliced into Robinson's chest so hard the point came out his back. Amazingly, the dead body stayed sitting in the saddle as his horse continued running.

Two more eager riders had come plunging up the slope with Robinson. Fargo skinned his Colt just as Megan and Julius also opened fire. One man slumped dead and slid off his horse, while the other caught a slug in his belly and retreated, howling.

"Cease fire!" Fargo barked. They were all critically low on ammo now.

"We did it, Skye!" Julius exalted. "Turned them back!"

"Yeah, but we can't do it again," Fargo reminded him, "and here comes the main gather."

Bryce, no doubt sensing the defenders were low on ammo, had continued the charge despite the fate of his advance riders. They streamed up the lower part of the slope, guns cracking like whips.

Fargo had to dangerously expose himself to fire in order to align the Henry's sight with those nitro blocks. Seeing all those killers, worked up to a frenzy like Viking berserkers, turned Fargo's stomach into a ball of ice. And here he was, counting on 'expired munitions' to save their bacon.

"Skye!" Megan cried, on the feather edge of hysteria. "Why are you waiting? They're on the slope!"

"Calm down, girl. We need to wait until more of them are near those blocks. If the first one blows too soon, they'll turn back."

"*If* it blows—you got that right," Julius said in a voice tight with fear.

With riders pounding closer, Fargo slipped his finger inside the Henry's trigger guard and curled it around the trigger. He brought the front sight down on the yellowish nitro block hidden behind the rock. Fargo took up the slack, squeezed evenly, and felt the Henry kick into his shoulder socket.

The bullet punched squarely into the block, so hard the nitro leaped. Nothing. Fargo felt his heart turn over—they were down to bedrock and showing damn little color.

"Aww, *Christ!*" Julius swore. "God*damn* it! That was our only chance."

Fargo, however, rarely folded until he'd seen his hole card. With bullets fanning his hair, he swung the Henry's muzzle to the second block.

"Why bother?" Julius said bitterly as Fargo squeezed off one of his last rounds. "We're all goners—"

The deafening explosion from the slope was like the last crack-boom of Doomsday. For a moment, before Fargo himself was knocked senseless, he saw men, still astride their horses, outlined against the sky. Much of the slope disappeared in the fiery explosion, raining down on the ridge.

Then something hard banged into Fargo's forehead, and the world ceased to exist.

.

22

"Skye! Skye, wake up! There's more trouble coming!"

Fargo heard a canteen cap being untwisted, and water splashed in his face. His eyelids eased slowly open. His head throbbed like Pawnee war drums.

Megan's frightened face hovered over him. "Skye, thank God! We thought you might be dead."

"I *might* be," Fargo replied, groaning as he sat up. Gingerly, he felt the goose egg on his forehead.

"Situation's still dire," Julius reported tersely. "That explosion put about half of the Jayhawkers out of the fight. But the rest are massing below for some kind of action. And they look *mad*—all horns and rattles."

Fargo's eyes finally focused on the ruined slope and the men beyond it. These vigilantes might be moral trash, but clearly they weren't afraid to scrap. He watched the grim-faced men reloading. Neither Reed McKinney nor 'Bama Jones was among the dead on the slope or their living comrades. That bothered Fargo.

"It's clear what they'll do," he said. "They'll come up the slope to our right, then hook toward us through the trees. We can't make a stand without ammo, but at least there's one toss-pot left."

Julius cleared his throat. "Actually, it's a dud," he confessed, eyes fleeing from Fargo's. "Two of the six were. They'll throw plenty of sparks, like the one last night, but no explosion. I meant to palm those two off on some ignorant criminals."

"The whole world and every soul in it," Fargo muttered, "crazy as loons. Good thing I didn't grab one of them back in Miller's Bend or we'd *all* be doing the hurt dance. All right, it's too dead to skin. Let's get those hobbles off the horses. We'll make a run for it."

"But the horses," Megan balked. "They're tired."

"Done in," Fargo agreed. "Just like we'll be if we stay here. I'm prac'ly out of bullets and so are you two. I'd rather take my chances in a running battle."

However, the Jayhawkers chose that moment to move to a new section of the grassy slope and begin their ride up to the crest of the ridge.

"No time to escape now," Fargo said, his crop-bearded lower jaw jutting hard. "Let's move out ahead of our horses or they'll be slaughtered. We'll make our stand in the trees. *Listen* to me, both of you. Stand sideways behind a tree to reduce your target. Don't panic and jerk your triggers. Breathe slow and deep, and *squeeeeze* that trigger so you don't buck your shots. Every bullet has to count."

Despite his calm, confident exterior, the Trailsman never fooled himself. Ten to three wasn't impossible odds—Fargo had faced worse. But in a lead-tossing contest, you had to have plenty of lead. These thugs were bristling with ammo, and Fargo feared three more souls would soon cross the River Jordan, his among them. His enemies, however, would pay dearly so long as he had an ounce of fight left in him.

They moved out ahead of the horses, watching from the trees as the riders surged closer. Fargo had seen Nat Bryce among the dead on the slope. A hard twist with a livid knife scar on his right cheek led the action.

"Megan, I love you," her father said gruffly. "I'm sorry I got you into this."

"I'm sorry you did, too," she replied. "But I love you too."

That exchange unnerved Fargo more than the advancing men did. If the snarling Kinkaids were reduced to such loving talk, it *had* to be curtains for all three of them.

A faint drumming from the northwest caught Fargo's ear. The rataplan of galloping hooves. When the stirring bugle notes of the cavalry charge reached his ears, Fargo almost found religion.

"The Beardslee," he explained to the other two.

"Whoever has it heard the fight here and alerted soldiers."

The Jayhawkers, too, heard the approaching soldiers and wanted no part of a clash with the regular army. The guerrillas would be hanged for treason. They turned down off the slope and fled to the south.

"We better raise dust, too," Fargo advised, hurrying back to the horses. "I have friends in the army, but I don't want to explain that ruined slope and those dead Jayhawkers. Not to mention we're all outlaws on the dodge. If we slip down the east side of the ridge and follow the river, they won't even see us. They'll be chasing Jayhawkers."

"Kansas City, here we come!" Julius celebrated as the trio rode out. "By God, no dime novel ever written could be like this true adventure alongside the Trailsman. Fargo, I suspect bees will not sting you."

"I've been bee-stung, snake-bit, and plagued by the squitters," Fargo assured him. "Right now, though, I'm more worried as to the whereabouts of Reed and 'Bama."

Megan paled. "They didn't die on the slope?"

"Nope. And they weren't among the survivors. So they're most likely around here somewhere."

Against Megan's will, a tear spurted down her cheek. "It's just not *fair*! We survived a gun battle up north, that terrible trap in Miller's Bend, the attacks on the plains, that near miss in Johnson City—when will it ever end?"

"Actually," Fargo replied, squinting to see better in the glare of morning sunlight, "it might have already ended."

Shoots Left-handed rode toward them, one hand held up to show he approached with no weapon.

"It is done," he told Fargo. "Behold the mighty butchers of the *Shayiela* women and children."

Megan screamed, Julius goggled, and Fargo merely stared without emotion when the Cheyenne subchief raised two human heads into view, severed raggedly at the necks. Both bounty hunters' faces had frozen in a look of agonizing death.

"After the big thunder on the ridge," the brave explained to Fargo, "they ran away like cowardly Poncas. Right into the path of my iron-tipped arrows. I left their bodies for carrion, but first I took enough skin from each to make a parfleche."

"*Ipewa,*" Fargo told him. "Good. Now the sacred arrows can be cleansed of blood and renewed. He who died beside you did not die in vain."

"Son of Light, our women will sing your deeds and the children will grow up knowing about the brave and honorable *mah-ish-ta-shee-da* named Fargo."

It was not the Indian way to indulge in good-byes. Shoots Left-handed wheeled his pony and rode to the north, both heads bouncing against his saddle.

"This isn't just luxury," Megan said with a contented sigh. "It's the top floor of heaven. Father and I are seriously thinking about staying here in Kansas City."

Fargo, well scrubbed and well fed, stood in a bay window of the Commerce Hotel, fifth story. He watched a train ease into town along a westbound spur, hissing to a steaming stop when the engineer vented his boilers.

"Why not?" he agreed. "Just be sure to use summer names for awhile, and for Christ sakes, *no* French accents."

Since they wouldn't be needing their mounts, the Kinkaids had sold their horses to a livery for a tidy sum. Megan finally had her new dress, and much else besides. She also insisted on rooms in the best hotel in town, replete with fleur-de-lis wallpaper and pillows thick with satin stitch and French knots.

"Speaking of staying here," Fargo said, turning around to gaze at both of them, "I do hope, Julius, you still plan to live on the street called Straight?"

"Absolutely, Fargo. But I'm putting off that teaching job to write my next novel: *Death on the Plains, a Saga of the Trailsman.*"

Fargo scowled, and Megan quickly spoke up. "He finally realized that you're famous out west. Now he hopes to cash in. It's his nature, Skye, and he'll never change."

Fargo surrendered with a grin. "Well, writing is *almost* honest labor, I s'pose. Uh, Julius, that's Skye with an 'e.' "

Three raps at the door sent Fargo's palm to the walnut grips of his Colt. However, it was only a porter with a telegram for him from the Grangers Bank in Plum Creek. It was this reply that had delayed Fargo's departure from Kansas City.

"I telegraphed them the day after we got here," he explained. "I got to worrying that *Sheriff* Brubaker back in Miller's Bend might have sent men after the express rider."

Fargo tore open the yellow Western Union flimsy, his face breaking into a toothy grin as he read the lines. He looked at the Kinkaids.

"Good news?" Julius prompted.

"You know, thanks to you two reprobates, this whole adventure was money down the drainpipe for me. But that's changed."

He looked at the telegram and read aloud, " 'We have received the money you sent and notified the Grangers Bank in Kansas City to pay you the sum of ninety dollars, our standard ten percent finder's fee.' "

Megan clapped excitedly.

"Oh, there's more," Fargo assured her, his eyes watching Julius until he started reading again. " 'We never suspected you of robbing our bank, Mr. Fargo, despite the rumors. All wanted posters for you, printed without our knowledge, have been pulled. If a man like you robbed a bank, he'd do it openly, gun in hand. This was sneak-thievery with more cunning than courage.' "

"Sneak-thievery requires plenty of courage," Julius sputtered. "The man's an ass."

Megan watched Fargo tuck the telegram into his shirt pocket. Her pretty face formed a pout. "Don't tell me—the eternal wanderer is going to pick up his money and ride off into the sunset?"

Fargo nodded, giving her a lingering hug that picked her right up off the floor. Then he shook Julius's hand.

"But *where* are you going, Skye?" Megan called as his rein-callused hand gripped the fancy glass doorknob.

Fargo sent her a cross-shoulder glance. "West," he replied. "Always west."

LOOKING FORWARD!
**The following is the opening
section of the next novel in the exciting**
Trailsman **series from Signet:**

**THE TRAILSMAN #302
BLACK ROCK PASS**

*Utah Territory, 1860—where the pony express
has linked one side of the continent with the
other, but the only way to bridge the gap between
good men and bad is with hot lead.*

The sound of gunfire made the lake blue eyes of the big
man in buckskins narrow with suspicion. In this rugged
land through which he rode on the magnificent black-
and-white Ovaro, a sudden outbreak of shots was almost
never a good thing.

Skye Fargo reined the stallion to a halt. He was about
halfway up a ridge dotted with scrubby juniper trees,
and the gunfire came from somewhere on the other side.
Fargo wasn't the sort of man who ran from trouble, so
as soon as he had pulled the Henry rifle from its saddle
sheath, he heeled the Ovaro into motion again and rode
quickly to the top of the slope.

He stopped again there to take stock of the situation.
The ridge fell away before him to a broad, flat stretch
of semi-arid land. A lone man on horseback was gallop-

ing from east to west along there, twisting in the saddle from time to time to trigger more shots at a knot of riders about fifty yards behind him.

The pursuers rode ugly little ponies that were faster than they looked like they ought to be. They wore buckskins, feathers, and war paint.

Fargo's jaw tightened as he recognized the Indians as Paiute warriors. The Paiutes had gotten along peacefully with the settlers at times in the past, but like most of the tribes they had eventually gotten tired of the white man's ways and become more war-like.

These Paiutes were doing their damnedest to catch that lone rider, and if they did, what they had in mind for him probably wouldn't be too pleasant.

Down below on the plain, the fleeing man must have emptied the pistol in his hand, because he jammed it back in a holster and drew another revolver from his saddlebags. He turned to fire. His shots weren't doing any good, though. The Paiutes never slowed down.

Fargo lifted the Henry to his shoulder. The distance was about three hundred yards, not an easy shot, but not too difficult, either, at least not for him. He aimed, held his breath, and squeezed the trigger.

The pony ridden by the warrior who was in the lead stumbled and then collapsed as Fargo's bullet struck it in the chest. Fargo hated having to kill the horse, but the alternative was to shoot the Indian, and he wanted to do that even less.

While the echoes of the first shot were still rolling over the landscape, Fargo worked the rifle's lever, shifted his aim, and fired again. A second horse went down, tossing its rider over its head. The Paiute flew through the air and crashed to the ground not far from where the first warrior had fallen when Fargo shot his horse out from under him.

The other three Indians began pulling back, unsure where the shots were coming from. One of the two who had been unhorsed ran after them, but the other warrior snatched up the rifle he had dropped when he fell. He lifted it and drew a bead on the still-fleeing rider.

Fargo said, "Damn," and jacked another round into the Henry's chamber. He hadn't figured on the Paiute being so blasted stubborn. He fired, but not in time to keep the warrior from pulling the trigger, too. Smoke geysered from the muzzle of the Paiute's rifle.

An instant later Fargo's bullet struck him and lifted him off his feet, throwing him backward. The warrior landed with arms and legs flopping in the boneless sprawl that signified death.

At the same time, the rider jerked in the saddle and sagged forward, but managed to hang on and keep riding. Fargo knew that the Paiute's final shot had struck the man. That last-ditch effort had found its target.

He turned to look at the rest of the war party. One of them had picked up the other man Fargo had set afoot, and now they were riding double. Dust boiled up from the hooves of the horses as the Paiutes took off for the tall and uncut. Obviously, they didn't want any part of the deadly accurate rifleman on top of the ridge.

Fargo lowered the Henry and then replaced it in the saddle sheath. He looked at the lone rider and saw that the man had slowed his horse to a trot. Whether or not that was deliberate, Fargo didn't know. He heeled the Ovaro into motion again and headed down the slope toward the wounded man.

The rider's horse came to a complete stop before Fargo could get there. The man swayed back and forth a couple of times and then pitched out of the saddle to fall heavily to the ground.

Fargo urged the stallion to a faster gait. By the time he reached the wounded man, the hombre's horse had wandered off a short distance and started cropping at the sparse grass. The man hadn't moved since he fell.

Fargo swung down quickly from the saddle and dropped to a knee beside the man, who lay facedown. Keeping one eye peeled for the Paiute war party, just in case the Indians decided to double back, Fargo carefully rolled the man onto his back.

He was more of a kid than a man, Fargo saw, probably

no more than seventeen or eighteen years old. Lank blond hair fell around a thin face. He wore buckskin trousers and a homespun shirt, and both back and front of that shirt were stained with blood. Fate had guided that hastily-fired bullet clean through him.

Fargo figured the youngster didn't have more than a few minutes to live. Anger made his jaw with its close-cropped dark beard clench hard. Violent death was always part of the frontier and was never far away, but it made Fargo mad when the victim was someone this young.

The youngster's eyelids flickered open. He stared up at Fargo without really seeming to see him at first. A thin line of blood trickled from the corner of his mouth. When his eyes finally focused, he asked hoarsely, "How . . . how bad . . . am I hurt?"

"Pretty bad, son," Fargo said as gently as he could. He started to stand up.

"D-don't go!" the youngster said desperately.

"Just getting my canteen," Fargo told him. "A drink of water might make you feel a little better." And it might ease the young man's passing, Fargo thought.

He fetched the canteen that hung from the Ovaro's saddle and then knelt beside the wounded man again, getting an arm around his shoulders and lifting him a little. Fargo propped the youngster against his knee and then held the mouth of the canteen to his lips. The young man sucked thirstily on it for a moment and then said, "Yeah . . . yeah, that's good. . . ."

"What's your name?" Fargo asked.

"B-Billy . . . Conners. I ride for . . . the Pony Express."

Fargo frowned. He wasn't too surprised by what Billy Conners had just told him. He knew that most of the riders for the recently established Pony Express were young men. "Orphans Preferred," in fact, was the way Russell, Majors & Waddell, the company that had started the mail delivery service, had advertised for employees. The company hired young, slender men whose weight wouldn't slow down the horses they rode. Billy Conners fit that description.

"I reckon that's a mail pouch on your horse," Fargo said.

"Y-yeah. Mister, I . . . I hate to ask it . . . but can you see the pouch through? Get it where it's . . . goin'?"

"Where's that?" Fargo asked.

"Next relay station is . . . Black Rock Pass . . . 'bout five miles . . . west o' here."

Fargo didn't hesitate. He nodded and said, "Yeah, Billy. I'll get the mail pouch to the station at Black Rock Pass. That is, if you can't deliver it yourself."

Despite the lines of pain etched on his face, a grim smile tugged at the corners of Billy Conners's mouth. "You ain't . . . much of a liar . . . mister. I know I . . . ain't gonna make it. That's why I 'preciate you . . . makin' sure the mail gets through."

"Rest easy on that score," Fargo assured him. "It'll get there."

Billy licked his lips, and Fargo gave him a little more water. The drink made him cough this time, and quite a bit of blood came up, flecking his chin and the front of his shirt. When the coughing spell passed, the youngster said, "Them damn Paiutes . . . come out of nowhere to jump me. I was . . . bein' careful. I've . . . rode this route . . . before."

"Sometimes it doesn't matter how careful you are," Fargo told him. "Things still catch up to you."

"Y-yeah." Billy blinked several times, and the life seemed to fade some in his brown eyes. But it hadn't gone out of them completely, and he forced himself to say, "M-mister . . . who are you?"

"My name's Skye Fargo."

Billy's eyes widened a little with pain or recognition or both. "F-Fargo . . ." he said. "Imagine th-that." He began to shake as if with a chill. "I get myself shot . . . and who comes along . . . to help me . . . but the Trailsman!"

A sudden, sharply indrawn breath hissed between his teeth, and his back arched a little. When the air came out of him with a sigh, the rest of Billy Conners's life came with it. A glassy haze settled over his unseeing eyes. Grimly, Fargo closed them.

Then he eased Billy's body to the ground and stood up. He had a promise to keep. He walked toward Billy's horse, talking quietly to it.

The animal started to shy away, and Fargo noticed that it was favoring one leg. That explained why the Indian ponies had been able to keep up. Normally the grain-fed mounts used by the Pony Express could outrun the grass-fed Indian ponies. Even though his horse hadn't yet gone lame, it wasn't able to run at full speed.

Fargo's soothing tones calmed the animal enough so that he was able to catch hold of its reins. Once the horse felt Fargo's hand on the reins it settled down even more. He unhooked the mail pouch that was strapped to the saddle and carried it over to the Ovaro, where he fastened it to his own saddle.

Then Fargo lifted Billy's body and carefully draped it over the back of the Pony Express horse. The youngster's light weight made it easy for Fargo to handle him. The smell of blood made the mount a little nervous again, but Fargo got the corpse tied in place.

He swung up onto the stallion and rode west, leading the Pony Express mount with its grim burden. A range of small, rounded peaks rose in front of him. Fargo had been through these parts before and knew they were called the Cricket Range. Black Rock Pass led through the mountains, and beyond it was desert that stretched to the Nevada border. Fargo hadn't known that a Pony Express relay station had been established at the pass, but he wasn't surprised.

Keeping an eye on his back-trail, he pushed on through the afternoon, leaving the flats and riding through increasingly rugged terrain. He saw no sign of the Paiutes following him, but that didn't mean they weren't back there. They would be unlikely to forget that he had killed one of the warriors and two horses. And they might have been part of an even larger band that was raiding through this southwestern corner of Utah Territory.

Excerpt from BLACK ROCK PASS

For a man like Fargo, whose keen eyes saw things that another man's might not have, the trail used by the Pony Express riders was easy to follow. It led him on a winding path through the mountains before emerging onto a long, straight, gradually declining slope. At the bottom of that slope, on the dividing line between mountains and desert, stood a couple of buildings. Fargo knew that had to be the location of the Black Rock Pass relay station.

No other series has this much historical action!

THE TRAILSMAN

S310

GRITTY HISTORICAL ACTION FROM

USA TODAY BESTSELLING AUTHOR

RALPH
COTTON

Available wherever books are sold or at
penguin.com